THE NATURE-PRINTER

THE NATURE-PRINTER

*A tale of industrial espionage,
ferns & roofing-lead*

Simon Prett
Inspired by the accounts of Pia Östlund

Foreword by Roderick Cave

TimPress
REIGATE

Published by
THE TIMPRESS
High Trees, Oaks Road, Reigate

Images on pages i-iii by permission of Chelsea Physic Garden Archive. Image on page xxii by permission of the Historical collection of the Department of Biodiversity Research (University of Vienna). Images on pages xxiv and xxv by permission of Designmuseum, Danmark. The Library. Image on page xxvii by permission of Arcane Studios. Photography on pages i, ii, xxvii and xxxii © and by permission of Andrew Montgomery. Original nature-prints, herbarium specimen, monoprint and photography on pages iii, xxii, xxiv-xxvi, xxviii and xxix-xxxi © of Pia Östlund. Photography on pages iv-xxi and xxiii by permission of Michael Hayward. Cover and text design by Tim Preston. Copyright of the text of this book belongs to Simon Prett & Tim Preston. Copyright of the Foreword belongs to Roderick Cave. Printed on Munken White, 80g. Text set in Justin Howes' ITC Founder's Caslon 12/15pt. Printed by GraphyCems in north-eastern Spain. Year of publication: 2016. ISBN 978-0-9934845-0-6

The copper engravings by Elizabeth Blackwell in *A Curious Herbal* (1737-9) and the paper mosaics by Mary Delany (which so entranced Queen Charlotte and Sir Joseph Banks) were landmarks in the evolution of image-making. Anna Atkins, another woman at the forefront of technical development, produced *Photographs of British Algae, Cyanotype Impressions* (1843-53), the first book ever illustrated photographically. Few others attempted this laborious process because another method of illustrating plants was emerging: naturselbstdruck as the Austrians called it; phytoglyphy as named by the English hero (or villain) Henry Bradbury. We now remember it as nature-printing and for a few years it was used to illustrate some very beautiful books.

As early as 1900 some book artists were looking backwards and trying to emulate the work of the Victorians. The revival of wood-engraving, the improvement of typography – even what seems very simple and straightforward, how to damp paper to aid presswork – had to be rediscovered. Many print historians have read about the processes and moved on. Pia Östlund has not been content to simply read about it. Just as Anna Atkins learned about cyanotyping from Herschel and transformed herself into a chemist and photographer to making printing her book possible, Pia has steadily re-created a complex printing technique which disappeared a century and a half ago. That in itself is remarkable, as Simon Prett's book shows. But The Nature-Printer is not just a celebration of her work: it tells again the extraordinary story of industrial espionage (worthy of Wilkie Collins) and makes clear that nature-printing is still much more than a typographical curiosity.

RODERICK CAVE

As part of her job at Chelsea Physic Garden Pia sometimes gets to run a short course on nature-printing, which is a method of printing directly or indirectly from something like a feather or a leaf. This is why, on a warm morning in early summer, she stands facing a small group in a sparsely furnished room with the comfortable atmosphere of a village hall. On a table in front of her are two volumes from the tiny library next door. Shafts of sunlight drop through high windows and filter the dust. As one of the members of the group I find my attention wandering to the small garden that was established here in 1673.

The first book we're shown, probably a singleton prepared by Joseph Miller during his tenure as head gardener some sixty years later, consists of prints taken directly from plants in the Garden and so in a sense it *was* the Garden in 1730. These prints provided a true representation of plants at a time when there were few alternatives. The traditional herbarium – dried specimens mounted on sheets – was both fragile and cumbersome, while artistic representations in the form of botanical illustrations and engravings were not necessarily accurate. Miller's prints are remarkably well-made directly from the inked parts of plants. The pages are printed on both sides and the prints have been hand-coloured. They are exactly what I would expect prints from plants to look like: dark in some places, light in others, with some fuzziness in the detail.

The second, an elephant-folio called *The Ferns of Great Britain and Ireland Nature-Printed by Henry Bradbury*, takes us by surprise. As the text was provided by Thomas Moore, one of the curators of Chelsea Physic Garden, it has a special connection with this place. Doubtless he also co-ordinated the collection of specimens. We are looking at images that are more than 160 years old and there is a perfect delicacy of colouring on the pinnules of each frond, a breathtaking detail of venation on the sharp-toothed mittens of *Polystichum setiferum*. There is a general sense of wonder. How is this possible? Pia tells us this is how she felt when she opened the book and over the past few years her goal has been to find the answer. At this point she takes a small tissue-wrapped plate out of her bag and the print made from it of an oak leaf, and passes both around. This is her endeavour, the result of years of extra-mural research. There are murmurs of warm appreciation and her polished, tin-backed copper-plate is handled as if it is a precious object. Someone compares the skeletal pattern of the oak leaf with a fine crackle glaze. We are not able to attempt such work today, but the books prove to be an inspiration. If anyone was in any doubt, they realise now that nature-printing is a fine art (and not, as I imagined, a primary school activity involving potatoes and squeezy bottles filled with poster paints).

There's just one more picture she wants to show before we begin. It is the print of a small bat taken from a Viennese book published in 1855. Think of a ball of fur with splayed arms and legs, in line with the basic human template, except the length of the fore-arm from the wrist to the elbow is twice the length of the upper arm from elbow to shoulder. The thighs are short, the toes are proportionate for the legs and feet and likewise the hooked thumbs for the arms; but the elegant fingers are impossibly long, like spokes for the webbed wings with their exquisite tracery of blood vessels. The image sits above the surface of the paper and has a texture that makes it seem more real. It's hard to believe this is a 'nature-print' but it demonstrates what has been achieved. On first seeing this image in a magazine called *Faust* the writer Naomi Hume asked 'what kind of bargain must the printer have made to achieve an image of such lifelike and unchanged longevity?'.

Nature-printing has existed in the margins for centuries, as if no-one is quite sure what to make of it. It's easy to conclude, like the bat in Aesop's fable, that 'he who is neither one thing nor the other has no friends'. When I asked John Randle, publisher of *Matrix*, the definitive journal for private and small presses, why so little nature-printing had appeared in its pages, he dismissed the subject as a curiosity. These days, though, bats have plenty of friends, with over one hundred local bat groups in the UK alone. Perhaps it's also time for a reassessment of the status of nature-printing.

This is Pia's reason for agreeing to work with me, though I must admit to other motives. It seems admirable that she is determined to succeed at something so difficult and time-consuming. In comparison, much contemporary artistic activity appears careless, populist enterprise. The quality of her work speaks for itself. Abstract qualities from the lively backstory of nature-printing (like ambition, deceit, despair) have an obvious allure. Moreover, the form of nature-printing with which this book is concerned is one that appears to achieve a rare fusion of science, art and industry. Let's see how far we can stretch this point. On the other hand, in any area but particularly in print and production, *mutatis mutandis*, what is the point in pursuing redundant technologies (or, if you like, curiosities) other than as an exercise in nostalgia? Unless. Is it possible that an abandoned idea, one that fails to meet specific requirements, might turn out to be perfect in some other context? If there is a place for the conservation of ideas, it must be a book. Finally there is the journey itself, which takes in some seldom-visited places and views in search of the secrets of Bradbury's technique. Pia's quest had to be fitted-in around the job, taking longer than might appear here. Faults, misrepresentations, rambles and circumlocutions are my responsibility. Names of some characters have been changed.

SIMON PRETT

The decision to become involved with nature-printing came by chance at the end of a long day after Pia, who had gone to the Garden's library to check a name, found herself immersed in Bradbury's book. The prints were not just beautiful, they were a mystery. How were they made? A brief scan online revealed few facts. It soon became clear no-one was making images like this, an unexpected discovery which struck her with the force of a challenge.

Later the same evening Rosie Atkins, the Curator of the Physic Garden, took her final round of the building and found Pia still in the library. Together they examined Bradbury's work. Rosie, in her usual direct and positive way, suggested Pia find out how it was done then make her own prints. The decision had been made, already. To celebrate the moment they went for a drink. Doubts were soon dispelled. On the tube on the way home Pia smiled as if she had a great secret that could not be revealed to anyone. Here was something special that she could do, something no-one else knew about: discover the way to make sublime prints. How? She didn't have a clue.

* * *

The St Bride Foundation occupies a tall red-brick building just south of Fleet Street, close by the place where Wynkyn de Worde, England's first popular printer, established his press at the sign of the Sun in 1500. De Worde, who had been the foreman of Caxton's press, inherited all Caxton's printing materials. Instead of continuing to print books for the wealthy, as Caxton had done, De Worde turned to the production of cheap books for the mass market: romances in prose and verse, riddles, almanacs, grammars and books on etiquette. The library at St Bride's holds a collection of Caxton and De Worde as well as over sixty thousand books, catalogues and magazines devoted to the various arts of printing – on presses, type and typography, graphic design, lithography, papermaking, calligraphy. Very few of these make any reference to nature-printing but thanks to the support of the Assistant Librarian, a picture begins to emerge; and in a small book bound in black cloth, *Die Entdeckung des Naturselbstdruckes* (*The Discovery of the Natural Printing-Process*) is a detailed explanation:

> The object, be it a plant, an insect, or some pattern of weaving and the like, that is not subject to any hurt by pressure, is, when painted over with some tincture, to be put between an even polished plate of copper or of steel and a like one of lead, and after being made to pass through the rolling of a chalcographic press, that acts with a pressure of from 800 to 1000 hundredweight. When the two plates are disjoined, you see the object stamped into the leaden plate with a perfect resemblance to nature, and for the print one can make use of the respective colours as it is customary with engravings.

Even for an experienced designer like Pia, who works closely with printers, the passage is abstruse. Tincture of what? A what-o-graphic press? How much pressure is 1000 hundredweight? If lead can be found, how thick should it be? All the details are missing. The Assistant Librarian is at her shoulder. 'You see something old and it feels completely out of reach. It's so complicated you couldn't do it today.' It would be hard to disagree and Pia doesn't try, but this is the moment when her massing doubts dissipate; a vote of no confidence has blown them away.

Leaving St Bride's, she sees a notice for the forthcoming AGM of the Printing Historical Society and it registers because she has just finished a brilliant scholarly article by Elizabeth M Harris on nature-printing in the *Journal of the Printing Historical Society.*

Harris accounts for the growing reputation of the process through the 1850s by suggesting:

...the name 'nature-printing' became a label of respectability implying that some mechanical operation, however insignificant, in the production of a print had given it greater accuracy and fidelity to the original than there could have been in an ordinary print drawn and engraved by hand.

Here can be seen the printer's faith in progress. New ways of working have been introduced often over the last two hundred years, always with the promise that the quality of output will be unaffected or improved. Remember the desk-top publishing hiatus that spelled (often in Comic Sans) the end of type-setting? Or computer-to-plate technologies that replaced repro houses and planning departments with a large grey box? Printing is an industry that, like others, has always looked to reduce costs by replacing men with machinery. The version of nature-printing that interests Pia is precisely such an innovation, offering the familiar justification of qualitative improvements; in this case over illustration and engraving. Henry Bradbury, the printer of the book of ferns mentioned in the introduction, argued that:

the great defect of all pictorial representations of botanical figures lies in the inability of art to represent faithfully those minute peculiarities, by which natural objects are often best distinguished.

The implication is that nature-printing is an accurate objective mechanism, one that delivers images of things as they are without interference. Botanical illustration today is flourishing and even engraving has a place, albeit small, in the work of private presses. Whatever happened to Bradbury's nature-printing? It sounds good – so what went wrong?

The Victorian interest in ferns is a peculiar phenomenon that hasn't received much attention, according to David Elliston Allen, because it 'lies in a cultural no-man's-land, wedged uncomfortably – and discomfortingly – between the history of taste and the history of science'. This places it in the same region as nature-printing. Caroline, a friend and field-botanist who is also a member of the Fern Society, believes developments in nature-printing may have been a bi-product of 'pteridomania', the mid-Victorian fern craze. The two are linked by Bradbury's book.

When Pia visits Caroline in Reigate she is shown a copy of Thomas Moore's first book, *A Handbook of British Ferns* published in 1848, when he was twenty-seven. Ferns had captured the imagination of botanists and gardeners already but this book helped, more than any other, to raise the level of public interest. It caught the wave at exactly the right moment and was a runaway success. And here is another book, *Where to Find Ferns*, published towards the end of the Nineteenth Century. The author, Francis George Heath, suggests:

> Fern-hunting, to lovers of ferns, is one of the most delightful of pastimes. It gives zest to any country walk, because it adds the attraction of a hobby to the pleasure of being out of doors. Life, in the present age, is far too sedentary, and there exists too great a tendency to sit in rooms with closed doors and windows. Some people seem almost to dread air in motion, and they become, in time, so little used to it that, at length, the body itself is brought into a morbid state, currents of air become 'draughts' and cold and illness are the result.

That hectoring tone, characteristic of the age, persuades them to leave the house and visit a nearby copse even though it is quite late in the day and there is an imminent threat of rain. At the top of Evesham Road, where it joins Albion Road, Caroline points out a beautiful small fern, *Asplenium ceterach* (Rustyback), growing in the cracks of mortar on an old brick wall beside a Victorian house. They count more than fifty individual plants. It would have been easy to have missed them altogether. This is one of the special things about ferns. Though they are, as Moore says, 'objects of exquisite elegance', they grow unobtrusively all over the place. Caroline fears for the future of this colony. The house is being refurbished and the wall likely to fall victim to gentrification.

When they reach Colley Copse, it begins to rain hard. Pia puts up her hood and keeps her head down while Caroline introduces *Polystichum aculeatum* (Hard Shield fern) and *Polystichum setiferum* (Soft Shield fern) and explains how to tell the difference between the two. They find *Dryopteris dilatata* (Broad Buckler fern) and *Dryopteris filix-mas* (Male fern) and several magnificent examples of *Asplenium scolopendrium* (Hart's Tongue fern) beside a small stream. Caroline notes the position of each plant for the Surrey Botanical Survey. The hunt and the taking of a register are routine for naturalists and collectors. Pia begins to get interested and stops to inspect another plant. When she looks up, Caroline has disappeared. In the gloomy half-light it is fifteen minutes before they find each other.

This year the AGM of the Printing Historical Society is held at The Society of Antiquaries in Burlington House. Grand surroundings for a low-key affair. The attendees are academics; no-one from the commercial world has anything to learn from history. Following a report on the Society's activities – details on grants and prizes, finances and the election of officers – proceedings are closed formally and there is a short break before the new chairman presents an erudite and not especially seditious paper on the revolutionary history of printing. After all this it is time for tea and biscuits. And for Pia, it is also time for her first break.

It seems that here, everyone she talks to knows at least something about nature-printing. One person even asks her if she has ever attempted to print fish. She has not, but is aware of this unusual form of nature-printing which originated in Japan and goes by the name of gyotaku (from gyo 'fish' and taku 'rubbing'). It can be traced back to fishermen who worked as printers in the off-season. The fish is inked and pressure applied with the fingers to a sheet of paper or cloth that has been laid on its surface.

Eventually she meets Michael Twyman, a genial lecturer from the University of Reading. He admits to knowing a little about nature-printing. It turns out that Elizabeth Harris, the author of that brilliant article on nature-printing, is one of his old students; he supervised her dissertation on the subject. Michael does not believe that anyone has managed to reproduce the method that interests Pia in recent times, though he knows of someone at the Enschedé Institute who has tried and failed. He mentions a chemist based in Mainz called Peter Heilmann who has written extensively on nature-printing and is a great maker and collector of nature-prints. Finally he recommends a new book on the history of nature-printing by Roderick Cave, probably the world expert on the subject.

Later the same evening she re-reads the notes that she has made from Elizabeth Harris's work and, in particular, Harris's careful account of the dispute that arose concerning ownership of the process. The protagonists are familiar already. In one corner stands Henry Bradbury, responsible for the book of ferns at Chelsea Physic Garden; in the other is Alois Auer – Director of the Staatsdruckerei, the State Printing-house in Vienna – whose confident, verbose account she had inspected in the St Bride library:

> of the discovery of the natural printing-process, an invention for creating by means of the Original itself – in a swift and simple manner – plates for printing copies of Plants, Materials, Lace, Embroideries, Originals or Copies, containing the most delicate profundities or elevations as not to be detected by the human eye.

Such controversy seems inevitable in the development of any process and it would be best to keep out of the argument as long as possible, on the basis that her own interest is technical rather than historical.

My Dear Sir...

Bradbury spent time in Vienna and there is epistolary evidence of the episode, beginning with several letters of recommendation. One from the consul to the Austrian Embassy, another from a publisher of foreign bibles by the name of Bagster. The third would have been particularly satisfying to Auer, as it came from the man who had been instrumental in awarding a council-medal to the Staatsdruckerei at the Great Exhibition:

> My dear Sir,
> I have the pleasure to introduce you to my friend Mr Bradbury, who has a desire to see the wonders of the Imperial States Printing Office. I can assure you, that any kindness or assistance shewn to him, will be esteemed as a personal obligation. I am, my dear Sir, Yours very truly, Thos. de la Rue
> Deputy chairman of Jury Class 17, Great Exhibition 1851.

Henry Bradbury, son of a successful publisher, was soon on a spree with a free pass to some of the most interesting places in Europe. After months at Vienna he travelled on to Prague, Berlin, Frankfurt, Brunswick (Braunschweig), Leipzig and Paris, returning to London the following year. While at Vienna he was given an introduction to many new printing processes and shown the latest invention, Naturselbstdruck.

And this is the thing that really captured his imagination. Easy to see why. In the eyes of an ambitious, knowledgeable young man it represents an opportunity. It is an entirely new form of commercial printing, unknown in England, of which the Viennese expect great things. Bradbury dashes off a letter in his slightly tortuous spidery script to Herr Alois Auer, Counsellor and Director of the Imperial Printing Establishment, Vienna:

Dear Sir,

I have the honour of addressing you, for the purpose of asking your special permission, to be allowed the opportunity of making myself acquainted, in a practical manner, with a certain process of printing facsimiles of dried flowers – an invention lately introduced by you in the above Establishment – an invention which possesses practical as well as scientific advantages.

In asking this special mark of favour, I wish frankly to inform you of my purpose for making for a more extensive acquaintance with this method – and that is, that I wish to be allowed to introduce it into our Establishment in London in as much as we have already a large field for the application of so valuable a discovery, as it appears to me to be for Botanical works.

In being then permitted to introduce it, my greatest pleasure and study would be, to fully acknowledge the said permission in every possible way.

And it would moreover be a matter of honour as well as interest, to protect the same, as much as possible, for becoming known. Taking this opportunity of thanking you for your extraordinary kindness, and also of testifying my great admiration for your wonderful Establishment. I have the honour to remain Yours very gratefully, Henry Bradbury

Auer was delighted by Bradbury's request, because this is exactly how he envisages the future for nature-printing and it vindicates the unusual decision he has made to cancel his patent of the process. As he says:

...our natural self-acting printing process will call forth a new era in the publication and figurative representation of artistical-scientific objects. Russia has given up Jacobi's application of the

galvanoplastic in the year 1837, and France the Daguerreotypy
for general use in the year 1839; Austria has now furnished a
worthy pendant to these two inventions.

Auer is convinced that the world will be forever grateful to Austria
for the discovery and for this reason is insistent that it is made freely
available. In his reply to Bradbury he makes this very clear.

Dear Sir
You have had occasion [over] several months, to become closely
acquainted not only with our establishment itself, but also
with the manner of its being managed and directed for general
purposes, as well as manifold application, to continual progress.
You will be aware, that the visiting of the establishment, and
the examination of the different branches, is generally permitted
with the greatest possible liberality; with you, this readiness
to communicate was augmented by the recommendation of
highly esteemed friends in England, to whom we are sincerely
obliged. I therefore hope and wish, that you will in every respect
be satisfied with your reception, as well as your stay in our
establishment.
    By the above communication, your last letter is for the most
part answered; nothing is left, but to relieve the maxim I have
attempted to pursue in similar cases, concerning the Imperial
establishment entrusted to my direction. In the same manner as
the experiments in the diverse graphic branches are – at request
– disinterestedly communicated to every honourable person,
so I wish on the other hand, that nobody else should abuse
such a communication as a monopoly, or in short: since the
establishment does not monopolize its own experiences, it cannot
permit the same to be done by others.
    I am very glad of having been able to serve you, and, at the

same time, to prove, how much I value the good opinion of these worthy gentlemen, that have so impartially acknowledged the accomplishment of our establishment in England. I am with much esteem Yours very truly, Auer

This gives Bradbury what he wants on terms that do not seem onerous. Auer comments later that Bradbury worked very hard to understand nature-printing, but found it difficult to the point that 'his instructors were nearly put out of patience'. If this appears uncharitable it is also true that while acquiring these skills, Bradbury's feelings towards his benefactor are altered. When he writes to thank Auer, Bradbury cannot resist offering his own observations.

My dear Sir

My stay in Vienna is now drawing to a close, and, satisfactory as it has been in all respects I must say I shall be glad to be once more on my homeward track. My object in visiting Vienna, was to have the advantage of seeing the exact state of the Printing Arts as carried on and practised in the Imperial and Government Printing Establishment − certainly the most extensive, the most artistic and scientific − in the World. Perhaps no Establishment has laboured more zealously to promote the various branches of Printing. And their success, if not at so practical an issue as other countries, is none the less brilliant.

While the Imperial and Government Establishment of Vienna carried the highest distinction of merit 'the Council Medal' at the ever memorable Great Exhibition of 1851, held in London − England and France were only too satisfied to be honoured with a Second Class Medal.

They are entitled to a great amount of praise for the liberal manner with which they lay open − almost invite, I might say − the mysteries of the Noble Art. Until etc, Henry Bradbury

The word 'practical' (meaning 'commercial') was a favourite with Bradbury. Here he implies that the Printing-office, subsidised by the fat Imperial purse, can afford to be unconcerned with ordinary matters of profit and loss because it operates outside the 'real world'. Is there also a suggestion that exploiting this access to unlimited resources amounts to profligacy? A disregard of economic considerations would be tantamount to bad management and this personal indictment, it seems, is the thanks Auer gets for playing the generous host. Auer comments:

> Here Mr Bradbury means to say that the Imperial Printing-office does not know how to make use of its experiences and improvements for practical life, that is to say for profit; – no, Mr Bradbury, the director knows this very well, but it is not the task of this imperial establishment to work – as it were – for 'profit' alone.

The ambition is to be the world's most innovative, technologically advanced print business. Any large printing house is a capital-intensive affair. By way of comparison take a present-day example. The British Printing Corporation was born from the merger of two long-established print groups (Hazell-Sun and Purnell) in 1963. It struggles from the outset, is bought by Robert Maxwell in 1981 and given a new name: The British Printing and Communications Corporation (BPCC). Other printers, including Odhams, are secured. The company continues to founder and eventually is subject to a management buy-out. Following another merger with Watmoughs, the Polestar Group is formed in 1998. More companies are acquired and Polestar describes itself now as 'Europe's largest independent print organisation'. The numbers are bewildering. In December 2006 Polestar managed to cut its total debt from approximately £814m (no-one knows the exact numbers) to £257m in a financial restructuring, a debt-for-equity swap, essentially a write-off for investors. According to the *Financial Times* its backers lost £700m. A slightly less drastic event occurred in 2008, when lenders again exchanged the majority of their debt for equity. And in April 2011, in a pre-pack sale to Sun Capital for £1 plus an undisclosed amount of its remaining £95m debt, the majority of Polestar's pension scheme was also written off. Today this privately owned commercial company that prints many of Europe's glossy magazines claims to be doing well – whatever that means.

The Printing-office in Vienna, funded by the government, was founded in 1804 to print government documents and bank notes. Under Auer's direction the business 'does well' in the sense that it grows larger, it becomes 'polygraphic'. As it flourishes its remit widens until it occupies the intellectual heart of the country. Few other printers in Austria or elsewhere have the resources to compete in any aspect of production and publishing. As Auer points out, 'in all other printing establishments the graphic arts are carried on separately, but all together are not nursed in any other establishment within or without Europe'. The Printing-office can, if it chooses, command a virtual monopoly. In practice, other presses are allowed to continue and even to benefit from its groundbreaking work. For example, a privately owned company prints and publishes journals generously illustrated with the special productions of the Staatsdruckerei (*Faust*, 1854-62, *Gutenberg* 1855-56 and *Kosmos* 1857-60). The company belongs to Auer's brother Michael, which raises other awkward questions.

The price of dominance must be high and the fact that the Printing-office provided all services free of charge for the Academy of Science did not help with the management of costs. There were also, admittedly, certain extravagances. To mark the retirement of four employees in 1857 Auer threw a party for three thousand guests. The State's Printing-office was a considerable financial burden. It is not difficult to envisage a scenario in which someone decides it might be a good idea to tighten the Imperial purse-strings.

At the Centre for Fine Print Research (CFPR), part of the University of West England (UWE), there is an investigation of another obsolete mid-Victorian printing process that requires lead plates, called Woodburytype. In its promotional literature the CFPR demonstrates a fondness for acronyms which, when combined with the cloudiness of the language, brings it closer to the world of financial services than education. Perhaps, as it says, this is a case of 'adapting to changing demands of the marketplace and the requirements of the user'. The emphasis placed on 'collaborative projects' and KTPs (Knowledge Transfer Partnerships) offers hope and Paul Thirkell, a research fellow at CFPR with an interest in marginalised and extinct 19th Century photomechanical printing techniques, has agreed to meet Pia. She arrives early, catches a bus to Clifton and strolls across Brunel's suspension bridge. On the towers Samaritans' notices 'Talk to us any time day or night' bring to mind the story of 22-year-old Sarah Henley; she survived a fall from the bridge in 1885 when her skirts acted as a parachute, allowing her to drift down serenely to the rest of her long life. Today the Avon Gorge is a magnificent sight with ribbons of rising mist that curl like smiles around that implausible tale.

On the wall in Paul's office are small portraits, continuous tone images resembling photographs but with uneven surfaces and a strange depth of colour that does not seem possible with any printer's ink. These are Woodburytype prints he has made with an eerie beauty that takes her by surprise. The method of production is related to nature-printing, as is clear from Woodbury's own summary in a letter published in *The British Journal of Photography*, 17 March, 1865.

A lead mould is obtained by exposing a sheet of bichromated gelatine behind a negative, and exposing to parallel rays of light; then washing away the undissolved portions and taking an electrotype cast in copper. This mould is then backed with gutta-percha and placed in a suitable press, having a sheet of plate glass, with strong springs, let into the back. Having greased the mould, a transparent mixture of gelatine, water and suitable colour is warmed, and a small quantity is poured on the centre of the mould. A sheet of paper is then laid on it, and the lid of the press bolted down. This, by exercising a steady pressure, squeezes all the superfluous colour out at the side; and on opening the press, the picture is taken off the mould, and in that state is in relief, which, however, dries down to be very slightly so.

Paul puts it differently. 'The best analogy I've come across involves mashed potatoes and gravy[1]. Take a plate of mash and smooth it flat with your knife. With a fork, make grooves and other marks. Pour gravy over this landscape. The depth of the gravy makes it darker in the deep ruts, while in shallow depressions it is almost transparent. In the Woodburytype process the mash is a lead plate; the gravy is warm, pigmented gelatin.' He makes it sound simple.

They stroll to the silent print room. Various items of equipment are ranged against the white walls, and tables occupy the centre. On a desk is a roll of roofing lead. Pia has brought some pressed plants and also some leaves that had caught her eye on her stroll through Leigh Woods earlier that morning. Paul shows her a large hydraulic press, designed originally for the production of wood laminates, which the university uses to print large-format linocuts. Suddenly, the idea of pressing leaves into heavy metal seems absurd. She lays fresh sycamore leaves on a square of lead and is not surprised when they are mashed in the press without having made any impression on the metal. The plate is wiped clean

---

1 http://www.alternativephotography.com/wp/processes/woodburytypes/ the-woodburytype-process

and they try again, this time with a dried, pressed oak leaf from London. Amazingly, it is a success. Paul examines the plate closely and says that they can probably print from it. The results are far from perfect because roofing lead is dirty and the blankets used to back-up the paper are rough, too. All of the prints are marked with scratches from the lead and are stained. No matter. They can move on from here, though it might be a little awkward. Pia is not a student and there is no obvious way for the CFPR to finance this particular KTP. Nevertheless, they part with a determination to investigate ways of funding the project.

* * *

On the train home she reads about Walter Bentley Woodbury. His life sounds like a *Boy's Own* adventure. As an eighteen-year-old he abandons a desk job as a civil engineer in the Manchester patent office to join the 1851 Melbourne gold rush, but arrives too late in Australia to profit from it. Impetuous Woodbury then spends two-thirds of his savings on a camera, even though he can't afford any of the essential materials for the taking of pictures. It lies like a promise in the bottom of his bag. He survives, gets a steady job as a draughtsman and masters the art of photography. After a while he throws in this job too and heads for Batavia (Java) where he sets up a studio with a British photographer called James Page. Woodbury's photographs of Australia, Borneo, Java and Sumatra – among the earliest taken – are highly prized. In 1863, he is forced by ill-health to return to England and in 1864 he patents the photomechanical reproduction process that bears his name (British patent 2338). He promotes various other inventions over the next twenty years, continues to struggle with his health and business concerns, and eventually he has a complete physical breakdown. Fellow photographers establish 'The Woodbury Fund' with the aim of supporting his family through his illness. More than three hundred pounds is donated, a considerable sum. The fund's committee notes with satisfaction that there is some improvement in his condition; this optimism turns out to be misplaced. In 1885, the same year that Sarah Henley descends to the soft Avon mud, Walter Woodbury dies as the result of a suspected overdose of laudanum. A note by his deathbed, partly in French, is mostly indecipherable. The last legible sentence is in English: 'My most intimate friends will quite understand'.

This is an age of discovery and Walter Woodbury one of many representatives of the times – from a poor background, of modest means, with sufficient energy and drive to take on the world-as-it-is and to break new ground. The confidence, curiosity and intensity of purpose add up to a special spirit, one that makes things happen. Pia studies her oak leaf print as the train hurries past Swindon and feels a renewed sense of determination.

* * *

Over the next few weeks it feels as if she, too, is taking on the world. Most institutions are unwilling to offer funds to an unknown artist attempting to rediscover a lost technique of printing that has been seen by relatively few people. And then a friend mentions that the European Commission is offering grants in support of its Year of Biodiversity campaign. A travelling exhibition of nature-printing might be just the thing to celebrate the EC's sustainability policies. The call for submissions must be answered by June. Only five weeks remain to decipher the application form. She calls Paul Thirkell with the good news, then looks further afield. In a strong letter to the Austrian Cultural Forum in London Pia quotes from Auer's hyperbolic address to the Imperial Academy of Sciences, Vienna, in 1853:

Three important moments are prominent in the history of
the civilisation of the nations with regard to the press – the
invention of writing – Gutenberg's artificial mode of

printing – and the discovery, how Nature itself furnishes a process for printing.

She points out that the Imperial Printing-office in Vienna was once at the forefront of the printing industry, a world leader. People came from all over to benefit from its expertise. She plans to revisit one of Auer's greatest inventions for an exhibition, a small portfolio of prints and a dedicated publication – and wonders if the Austrian Cultural Forum might like to be involved in the programme.

Funding would make things so much easier and piece by piece her proposal comes together, begins to feel less like an exercise in wishful thinking and more like a valid proposition, with the potential involvement of Chelsea Physic Garden and the St Bride Foundation as providers of exhibition spaces and even an offer of support from the beleaguered Austrian Cultural Forum. And then, at the last moment, things suddenly fall apart when it proves impossible to secure backing from – of all places – the Centre for Fine Print Research. Paul has done his best but the amount of money at stake is insufficient to make a Knowledge Transfer Partnership viable and for 'economic reasons' the CFPR withdraws one week before the submission deadline. There is no time to find an alternative partner and the application collapses with the resounding crash of an opportunity lost.

Auer's fortunes are bound to the times and they are strange times. His enthusiasm for languages makes him a good citizen of a multi-racial Empire. One of Auer's first major projects at the Staatsdruckerei (which he controls from 1841-1868) draws on both his typographic knowledge and his linguistic ability. He assembles a comprehensive collection of fonts and to illustrate its significance publishes *The Lord's Prayer* in 608 languages and dialects, using specialist character sets where required. This work in promoting oriental languages, though not beyond reproach, secures Auer's membership of the Academy of Sciences. His font library was built with a flagrant disregard for laws of copyright. This may not seem a heinous crime. Today, the nature of digital workflow makes it difficult to avoid acquiring typefaces and many designers possess fonts they have not paid for. In Auer's time, though, such acquisition was possible only as the result of a deliberate strategy. Auer employed punchcutters to make copies and also utilised the new galvanoplastic process to form matrices of fonts, where punches were not needed. More than twenty thousand matrices were made in this way.

Auer is pleased to note that the results are exact copies of the originals. Since the Staatsdruckerei has no right to copy, for example, the fonts of Plantin or Bodoni or of the Imprimerie Impériale, this is theft on a grand scale. Auer's justification, that 'the Establishment...copies for its own use only, and does not permit any galvanic production or copies to be used elsewhere,' rather misses the point.

Auer works through the Uprising in 1848, a revolution inspired by radical students and intellectuals in the name of the underwhelmed and exploited poor; prompted by the usual injustices of a reactionary government and exacerbated by the romance of nationalism (the boundaries of this vast Empire encompass Croats, Czechs, Italians, Slovaks, Serbs, Germans, Poles, Hungarians, Romanians, Slovenians and Ukrainians); an incompetent monarch; and a state treasury that is broke. After appeasement fails Ferdinand abdicates and the entire court does a runner to Salzburg. His successor, the eighteen-year-old Franz Joseph, takes a more forthright approach; reverses all concessions made in the direction of constitutional democracy in favour of the tried-and-untrusted method of imperial absolutism enforced at the point of a bayonet by an army comprised largely of the hitherto-mentioned exploited poor. To expedite matters in Hungary he enlists the help of Tsarist Russia and by the early 1850s the autocratic state is settling down uneasily to the idea of repressive business as usual. There are improvements to the education system and the peasants are emancipated, but such token gestures do not much dispel the dystopian atmosphere of censorship and surveillance. And then, just as things start to improve, there is a war in Crimea. Austria maintains an awkward neutrality throughout the conflict and in so doing fails to endear itself to either side. Consequently, when Piedmont-Sardinia provokes war in 1859 Austria finds itself without allies, is humiliated, cedes territory and loses influence in Italy. With no friends, a weak economy and an Empire on the verge of collapse, Franz Joseph feels change is necessary and in 1860 announces a new constitution that gives a central parliament some authority over matters of industry, commerce and finance. Auditors are roused but elsewhere this fails to have the desired effect; further concessions are demanded – and so on, the art of decline and fall, a slow-motion car-crash.

In these strange times the Staatsdruckerei becomes a world-class institution with a peerless reputation. Auer gains a knighthood and additional responsibilities, as befits a captain of industry, including control of the government paper mill and management of the imperial porcelain factory. There are quibbles over costs now and then but no serious issues and during the late fifties he has the backing of Baron von Brück, the finance minister. Around this period Auer publishes an essay (*Mein Dienstleben*) which reads like a kind of Awards Ceremony speech. He acknowledges all of the appreciation shown him by his supporters, a willingness to engage in self-promotional puff which provokes strong reactions; it seems Auer has enemies in high places and things begin to go wrong when Brück is (falsely) accused of having mismanaged funds during the war with Italy; soon after being relieved of his duties Brück commits suicide. On top of losing the man he sees as his main ally, what makes this especially galling for Auer is that a misprint in a newspaper article printed by the Staatsdruckerei gives the impression that Brück is guilty. Auer thought the typo was introduced deliberately by someone in order to humiliate *him*. Brück's successor, Ignaz von Plener, faces a serious financial crisis. Sacrifices have to be made and under straitened circumstances polygraphic ambitions must be curtailed. The Printing-office budget is slashed, leading to redundancies and departmental closures. Bureaucratic pressures mount on Auer. In a fit of pique in 1864 he pens a new section of *Mein Dienstleben*, of what he calls 'combat writing', full of accusations and bitterness:

> Enemies have destroyed my life and achievements...they have destroyed in a few months through ignorance and spite the work of a quarter of a century.

The whole reads like a sorry tale of ordinary office politics. Names are named. Ministers Schwarzwald and Gabriely come in for particular criticism; so does Baron Schlechta who, it is claimed, has planted spies in the Printing-office. Auer needs permission from the ministry to publish this diatribe and permission is refused. Furthermore, von Plener orders Auer to surrender the manuscript and galley proofs and to destroy the printed pamphlet. Auer accedes and notes regretfully in his diary that the work was not an accusation but a defence of his honour. Decades pass before

33

the original documents resurface in the imperial library (delivered, perhaps, before orders were given to destroy them). A few copies were printed, edited by chief librarian Dr Payer von Thurn and published by Auer's son, Dr Carl von Auer. Only one or two survive and maybe it is just as well that if Auer is remembered today it is for his achievements, and primarily for nature-printing, rather than for his grievances.

There was enough support for the failed application to suggest at least a polite level of interest in the subject and while Pia may not have got very far, she knows that she has covered some distance. The slightly grubby oak leaf print is evidence of that. And Gillian Barlow, a member of Chelsea Physic Garden's Florilegium Society and a fine botanical artist, is enthusiastic about the print. She suggests creating a herbarium of specimens and also points out that Moore and Bradbury's book of nature-printed ferns may not be so obscure, after all. She has met numerous pteridologists over the years in the Cool Fernery, a lean-to glasshouse on the western border of Chelsea Physic Garden, and several of them know the work.

The Cool Fernery was built in 1907 on the site of the original glasshouse, which went up during Thomas Moore's tenure in 1862. For Moore, as Curator, it was a light moment in dark times. For a number of years he had suffered a harsh, cost-cutting regime. The apothecaries were keen to restrict cultivation to hardy medicinal plants. There was also a proposal to drive a railway through the Garden and the Society of Apothecaries wanted to cash in, to be rid of an expensive burden. Unfortunately (for the apothecaries) the terms of the lease drawn up by Sir Hans Sloane prevented an easy disposal. Worst of all, through the letters column of a national newspaper, Moore was snarled-up in an argument with a local resident over public access to the Garden. As it turned out, the 1862 glasshouse represented a change of direction; new investment was forthcoming. The question of access took a little longer, but the Garden opened to the public – in 1983.

The original heated glasshouse was not constructed for ferns, as they were considered of limited use, but for 'interesting plants'. By the time it was built, Moore had quite a reputation as a pteridologist. He capitalised on the runaway success of the drab *A Handbook of British*

Ferns with a best-selling sequel, *A Popular History of British Ferns*, containing attractive hand-painted engravings and, in addition to botanical detail, some colourful anecdotes. For example, a 'traveller's tale' recounted by Moore:

> on an elevated, uncultivated salt plain, of vast extent, west of the
> Volga, grows a wonderful plant, with the shape and appearance
> of a lamb, having feet, head, and tail distinctly formed, and its
> skin covered with soft down. The 'lamb' grows upon a stalk
> about three feet high, the part by which it is sustained being
> a kind of navel; it turns about and bends to the herbage,
> which serves for food, and when the grass fails, it dries up
> and pines away.

A plausible hybrid for a people struggling to come to terms with the new theory of evolution by natural selection. Moore assures his readers that the Scythian lamb, or Barometz, the Vegetable lamb of Tartary, 'consists merely of the decumbent, shaggy rhizome of a fern'. There is no longer any place for tales: for the tree once found near Orkney with fruits that, on falling in water, became Barnacle geese; or for the mandrake (grown today in the Garden) that screamed so violently when pulled from the ground that it killed all those who heard it.

In his *Popular History* Moore explains how to select and preserve specimens for a herbarium. He provides details of alternative names for ferns. Most significantly, there are records of local places where ferns can be found – not with GPS precision, but with sufficient detail to inspire an expedition. In a reprise of Pia's outing with Caroline, *Asplenium fontanum* flourishes...

> on an old garden-wall at Tooting, Surrey, *D. Haigh*. (The wall has
> recently been cleaned, and the plants perhaps destroyed.)

At some point all wall-sites for *Asplenium fontanum* were destroyed. The fern may never have been native to Britain. Or it might – and then have been extirpated in Victorian times. Moore's book led directly to the destruction of many sites by collectors who, at the time, were less than circumspect about conservation.

The Cool Fernery is a pleasant shrine to ferns and a suitable monument to Thomas Moore; although Gillian believes that, as far as pteridologists are concerned, the finest tribute to both might just be *The Ferns of Great Britain and Ireland Nature-Printed by Henry Bradbury*.

The kettle starts to whistle. Pia pushes back her chair and trudges to the hob.

'Well, I think it *should* be difficult,' says her friend. 'I mean, if it's easy, if anyone can do it, what's the point?'

Pia has been trying without success to find a studio with a hydraulic press like the one at the Centre for Fine Print Research in Bristol. Surely, in a city the size of London, there has to be one? It seems there isn't. 'Maybe one press is as good as another,' she replies doubtfully, as she returns to the table with a mug of tea in each hand. This is how it goes, stops and starts, flickering doubts and gentle, encouraging nudges.

Most people are helpful. Like the old man in a corrugated iron hut at the entrance to the yard of a builders' merchant who takes time to direct her to an open shed where she finds rolls of lead flashing stacked on pallets. There is a surprising choice in width and length, but even the small 390mm x 3m roll barely two millimetres thick, weighs over fifty pounds. On the wraparound label is standard safety information (do not smoke, eat, or bite nails when handling lead; wear gloves and a mask) which she intends to follow to the letter; and odd facts (100% recyclable, melting point 357°c, density 11.34g per cubic cm) aimed at customers it is hard to imagine.

She takes a small section from her new roll of lead to the London Print Studio, a friendly artist-run community on the Harrow Road that does offer access to a hydraulic press, though it turns out to be a quite different proposition from the machine used in Bristol. The Beever, a small iron box with a lever on one side that reminds her of a one-armed bandit, is wedged in a corner beside a lithography press. The room is light and from where she stands there is a splendid view of the Paddington arm of the Great Union Canal. A Mute swan and three Canada geese glide past in the direction of Little Venice.

As a leaf makes an impression it should be possible to achieve results using more substantial material. In the hush of the studio she is soon absorbed in the attempt to print from a doily that belonged to her grandmother. The inspiration for Auer's development of the nature-printing process was lace displayed at the Great Exhibition and printed by William Taylor of Mount Street, Nottingham. In *Impressions of Nature*, the book recommended by Michael Twyman, Roderick Cave explains:

> Books with examples of cut lace pasted in were widely used, but the samples were fragile and quickly became creased and grubby.

Taylor's printed samples of white lace (the lace itself is not printed but is embossed in the paper and sits on a blue ground) offered an advantage not lost on Alois Auer – the chance to produce objective images that do not rely on the skills of the engraver, illustrator, or even (possibly) photographer. But there is a difficulty: how were the printing plates for Taylor's lace produced? When confronted with lace prints sent first by the Austrian consul, then separately by the Austrian Chamber of Commerce, his response is disingenuous:

> I withheld my opinion and merely remarked that the copying could be effected in a more simple and less expensive manner.

At the time Auer had a small problem keeping control of the printing works and only recently had fended off a proposition for a separate lithographic department 'for printing scientific objects to be represented figuratively' by implying there were better ways. He wanted to keep everything in-house under his direct control and those lace prints were just what he was looking for. But how *were* they made? Luckily for Auer, his print manager Andrew Worring conjured an answer out of his hat. Auer took great delight in describing how, at the next session of the Chamber of Commerce, he was able to lay a book of patterns before the members:

> to their very great surprise; they found the resemblance so deceptive, that they took them to be real lace, until, by touching and closely examining them, they convinced themselves that they were the production of the printing press.

It is hard to believe Worring's exhibits made such a good impression, not least because Pia struggles to make any impression at all with the Beever. After a couple of hours she decides a short walk is necessary. She stands on Wedlake Street Footbridge and follows the line of the canal as it curves in the general direction of Birmingham. A soft breeze. No birds. On the way back she notices a group of five or six boys outside the All Stars Boxing Gym and Youth Club, restless with sports bags and phones and bursts of loud laughter. The day wears on and no matter what she tries, she can not make any mark on the lead. A studio technician wanders over and confirms she is working 'at maximum pressure'. She continues stubbornly for a while, but this is not a situation where being stubborn makes any difference. It just won't work and by five, she has had enough.

Following up leads from the meeting of the Printing Historical Society does not bring immediate benefits. Elizabeth Harris writes to say she has retired from printing history and all scholarly pursuits, preferring to make goats' cheese on a farm in a remote area of Dorset. There is better news from Peter Heilmann. According to Roderick Cave, Heilmann is 'the most versatile nature-printer who has ever been' with 'the most extensive private collection ever formed on the topic'. Cave goes on to say:

> Heilmann is not only a collector and writer on the history of nature-printing, he has experimented personally with every process of nature-printing known to him.

Pia has received a typewritten note on a curious letterhead from Peter Norbert Heilmann – Gautor-Apotheke, the words set top-left in neatly letter-spaced Lydian, a graceful calligraphic italic designed in the late 1930s. At the right is a quaint coat of arms consisting of an extended lower-case h; the serif on the ascender is reversed to suggest a pennant; the letter arches like a bridge over water. Above the shoulder of the character is a single palmate leaf, like a star.

> Many thanks for your letter and I like to response all your questions very well. In ce moment I have some problems in my pharmacy. We cannot find a pharmacist since three years and that is the rea whilst I have not made any nature print since this 3 years. I would like to print on sunday or so but than I have to help my woman and my daughther with her two little girls (5 and 9 years).

The letter includes a copy of a book Heilmann has published in German about the printing office in Vienna. It does not contain any technical details. He proceeds to recommend the Nature-printing Society, offers to show his collection and to talk further. She senses that he does not want to let her down, but knows he is in his eighties and that it is quite a while since he made any nature-prints; and in any case, it will be difficult for her to get to Mainz in the near future.

* * *

Friends have recited a litany of symptoms of lead poisoning so often that Pia has them by heart: mood swings, headaches, insomnia, fatigue, reduced sensitivity, death. There are not many sources and using roofing lead for printing is a matter of necessity rather than choice. She would prefer to find a firm that can provide lead plates, but most manufacturers are large concerns working at an industrial level. Letters, phonecalls and emails to forty-one companies elicit two positive responses, including one from LeadAtom Europe Ltd, 'suppliers to nuclear establishments, hospitals, government agencies and universities'. The company is based in Gosport, next to Portsmouth.

In the workshop she learns how far lead has fallen from grace. The word plumber comes from the Latin for lead (plumbum) but plumbers have not been allowed to use lead piping since the 1970s. Children are no longer permitted to chew on lead toys. Artists cannot obtain paint containing either white lead carbonate or red lead oxide. Hunters and anglers are encouraged to find alternatives to lead shot. Make-up still contains unspeakable additives, but no longer any lead.

Bob, one of the directors, gestures at a bowl of sugar cubes. 'Romans used to sprinkle lead on their food,' he says, 'and they liked to ferment their wine in lead pots. Thought it improved the taste. They reckon lead poisoning contributed to the fall of the Roman Empire'. These days, in virtually every context, use of lead goes down like – well – a lead balloon. Lead is persona non grata. It has a serious image problem and it feels important to come up with a positive line, so Pia recalls

42

how Beatrice Warde, public relations manager at Monotype during the heyday of letterpress printing, coined an inspirational catchline for typesetters:

With my twenty-six soldiers of lead I shall conquer the world.

The impact of this message about the power of language is diminished by the virtual disappearance of hot metal type. Letterpress is now the preserve of a small band of shuffling amateurs. No-one wants lead. And yet, there must be markets.

'Oh yes,' laughs Bob. 'It's an essential component of over one billion car batteries. Almost all of it recycled. And lead protects thousands of miles of underwater cabling.'

'It also provides an effective radiation shield for things like X-ray machines.' This comes from Tony, another director at the meeting. She is taken on a tour, shown the furnace, the melting pot, the pipes that take away the deleterious fumes. On one wall is a rack of ladles, a domestic touch that would be homely but for the drills, the fly press, the cabling, drums and other unfamiliar tools. Tony explains that LeadAtom Europe Ltd specialises in various protective canisters and shields for the handling and transportation of nuclear material.

'We also do commercial stuff,' says Bob. 'Decorative drainwork. Lead soles for the boots of divers. All kinds of things.' What's more, they don't mind working with lead. 'Really, you just need to be sensible. Lead isn't absorbed through the skin. So wear the proper clothes. Make sure you don't breathe it in and wash your hands.'

None of their products requires lead to have the perfectly smooth and unblemished surface that she needs, but they give her the impression that this would not be an insoluble problem. It seems the main difficulty might be transport. Thin plates stacked edge-on will buckle and, if laid one on top of another, will be squashed. They examine the CFPR plate and smudgy print with a level of professional interest. Has she brought any leaves along? By chance, she has an envelope of maple keys collected at the weekend.

'Whirlybirds,' says Tony. 'Perfect.'

They have a small rolling mill, just under two metres tall, a floor-standing machine consisting of a single, motorised, height-adjustable steel roller between cast-iron plates on a steel bench. In a matter of moments, a maple key is sandwiched between a small sheet of lead and a sheet of steel and is run through the mill. The result beats anything she achieved on the Beever. The seed part of the samara has made a deep impression that might prove problematic when printing, but the detail in the papery wing is flawless.

Bob insists on a whistlestop tour of Gosport. 'It's obligatory,' says Tony, as he shakes her hand. They drive past various fortifications and buildings that used to belong to the military or the navy. The place has a slightly run-down feel, that yellow patina characteristic of some seaside towns. Bob points out the railway, tells her it closed in 1953. 'We may be the largest town in the country without a train station.'

At the ferry terminal he hands Pia a weighty souvenir, three lead plates laid between sheets of cardboard and wrapped in brown paper. There is a two-hour wait for the next train from Portsmouth, so she sits on a bench among beds of scrubby begonias and watches small yachts hurry out to sea. The garden she sits in is dedicated to those 'members of the Armed Forces, Merchant Navy and Civilians who gave their lives or were injured'. A ferry from Cherbourg appears on the horizon, looms large, glides past. An efficient-looking modern military vessel lies parallel to the harbour, brings to mind newsreel memories of flag-waving crowds from 1982. When it is time to head for the ferry she walks around a mosaic of the world set in the paving with the Falkland Islands and South Georgia picked out in scuffed gold.

Nineteenth Century scientists working with images regretted the degrees of separation introduced by illustrator and engraver and this desire for an image untouched by human hands represented an opportunity for printers to cut costs. One of the aspirations for nature-printing was that it would meet the requirement for an 'objective' image. Stripping away all interference, all intelligence, all interpretation – leaving only the thing itself.

It seems a fierce morality – or at least, a deep anxiety – drove this attempt to create a pure image. The headlong pace of change so undermined the notion of the permanence of scientific truth that scientists were no longer sure of anything. What was shown to be true today could be proved false tomorrow. The world was far more complex than thought. One surprising side-effect of progress is a loss of confidence, the failure of subjectivity. A sense of self-doubt that leaves science flailing, because what's the alternative? What did they know? How did they know what they knew? There were things they didn't know, they couldn't be trusted. Take the scientist out of the picture, too. In this context it is easy to understand the rise of faith in machines as a means to achieve impartiality, what became known as mechanical objectivity. A machine might produce an authentic image without the need for conjecture or interpretation. This was the platform on which Auer introduced nature-printing.

Incidentally, a photographic department existed in the printing establishment in Vienna at least two years before the invention of nature-printing, but the significance of photography – its strengths and shortcomings – had not been fully realised when Auer made his grand claim for nature-printing. If it was his belief that nature-printing was the best thing to happen since Gutenberg sliced words into moveable type, this may also have been inspired by his presumption that nature-printing was an Austrian invention.

Following Peter Heilmann's recommendation, Pia joins the Nature-Printing Society, which introduces the subject in a handbook:

> People have always been fascinated with nature. For those of us who appreciate art but cannot draw, it is inspirational to have Mother Nature do the drawing.

There are two hundred and eighty members in total and more than ninety per cent are based in America. The images reveal much good work, especially in the area of gyotaku – and many helpful tips ('If the fish oozes badly through the anus, you may need to gut the fish'). Little is of practical use to Pia. The nature-printing project stutters as the result of work pressures. And then there is a small breakthrough after a visit to another lead factory, in Dagenham.

The standard of living in East London where Pia lives has improved in relative terms since the turn of the century. In 1902, the Cheapside branch of Thomas Cook could arrange a tour of 'Darkest Africa' and 'Innermost Thibet' but would not organise a tour of the East End for Jack London. He made his own way to the 'Abyss' (where life expectancy was almost half that of the West End) and lived among the people, then wrote about the conditions of their lives. Among other things, he drew attention to the plight of workers in lead factories. For example, the grim case of Mary Ann Toler who 'three times became ill, and had to leave off work in the factory. Before she was nineteen she showed late symptoms of lead poisoning – had fits, frothed at the mouth, and died'. At the time Dagenham was a country village, several miles from the East End. Between the wars it became the site of Becontree, the largest public housing estate in the world intended originally for people from the East End who had to be moved somewhere to make way for slum clearance. A little later, the Dagenham marshes were occupied by Ford's car plant, complete with blast furnaces and power station. The District Line arrived in the Thirties. Companies such as Samuel Williams and Sons employed hundreds at the docks. In its heyday Dagenham was the new Far East success story, a hive of industry. Over the last twenty years most manufacturing has gone. Pia catches the overground, then strolls through featureless streets to an industrial estate.

'We're roofers,' says Managing Director Marcus Bowerbank, with a gentle smile. This is a little understated, given that past projects include Buckingham Palace, Windsor Castle and the British Museum. He suggests discussing her idea with Charlie, the foreman of the works. 'Let's hope he's in a good mood,' he sighs, as they descend to the factory floor, where some men in blue overalls are busy at benches with ornamental rainwater goods, while others pass by with a cursory nod.

'Won't work,' says Charlie, with conviction. In reply Pia takes a dried gingko leaf from Chelsea Physic Garden out of her notebook. They head for the fly-press, a bench-mounted machine for punching shapes in metal. Charlie lays the leaf on an A5-size lead tile under the press, attaches a steel plate to the screw and spins the T-lever. Moments later they are all able to admire the perfect impression of the fan-shaped leaf in the lead. To conceal any sign of triumph she explains the problem with lead is that the surface is flawed. No print she makes from this plate would be perfect.

'Steel wool,' says Charlie. There is a pause. He looks at Pia to see if more is necessary. 'Polish it up,' he growls. 'Start rough with a two or three, then work up to zero or double zero grade.'

'Wear protective clothing and a mask,' says Mr Bowerbank, glancing at Charlie, 'and if your project takes off, let us know. We can supply sheets and may be able to do something with the surface.' Later, Pia discovers the EU has identified six categories of chemical protective suit. The Type 5, designed specifically to protect against dust and used widely in the nuclear industry, seems appropriate. A friend looks over her shoulder. 'Isn't this all getting a little technical?' he says. 'I thought you just wanted to make some prints.'

During her summer break she comes across a fragile pamphlet in the National Art Library called *The Discovery of the Natural Printing-Process by LOUIS AUER*. The phrasing is ambiguous, perhaps deliberately so. Is Auer writing about the discovery? Or is he claiming the discovery? Those capital letters may be a clue. The new process out of Vienna was developed for printing lace to keep the Austrian Chamber of Commerce quiet but it is not long before someone (Auer's colleague, Professor Heidinger) suggests using it to print plants. This is duly attempted with such perfect results that Auer is able to play a trick on botanists:

Several such leaves were cut out – of course pasted on both sides, and that with the colour varying in front and back, the skeleton fitting in, and such was the effect that connoisseurs, when holding them in their hands and looking at them through the glass, did not take them to be printed leaves but natural ones.

In his own account Auer appeared supercilious when he said:

I remarked to them smilingly – "Truly these are impressions produced in an artificial manner."

That botanists would fail to distinguish between a printed leaf and a real one seems about as credible as the suggestion merchants are unable to distinguish between lace and paper – but he is excited. This is the moment when he thinks he is on to something. Has he found the way to kill off lithography, to dispense with illustrators, engravers and other expensive middlemen? Is it so obvious? To let the objects print themselves? He encourages Andrew Worring to apply for a patent and perhaps he helps with the wording. Worring surely gives more credit to Auer than he deserves, given that Auer's part in the discovery amounts to little more than asking his staff to come up with a good idea. Worring's declaration reads like a disavowal:

> I, the undersigned (Worring) do hereby declare, of my own free and uncompelled will, that the problem proposed in the month of June, 1849, and supported by COUNCILLOR AUER, Director of the Government printing-office, to form matrices for galvanic multiplication from originals, as fossil fish, for instance, by moulding in gutta-percha, after words by the persuasion of the Commercial Chamber at Vienna, from lace, etc, for the purposes of obtaining forms from which to print from the copper and printing process, I hereby declare that the said problem was only solved by me in consequence of Councillor Auer's exclusive instruction, and that I was only on this occasion induced to think of substituting, for the easier production of the copy, soft lead, instead of the indicated composition. I further more confirm, that I applied for an Austrian exclusive privilege on the 28th June, 1852, only according to the expressed wish of the said Councillor Auer, that I obtained it AD October 17, 1852, Z7698/H and that I received from him (Auer) the account for paying the taxes on work or the further charges, with the assurance that I should never be obliged to restore these amounts. I finally confirm that half of the invention, and of the right of its product, is due to my respected Chief, on account of his intellectual and material co-operation, which I conscientiously repeat herewith.

Auer's name appears four times in the text while humble Worring mentions his own name only once (in brackets). It is easy to picture the short figure of Councillor Auer leaning over the shoulder of his tall foreman, hunched at a desk. Worring is wearing blue overalls. He feels Auer's warm breath on his cheek as he chews his pen laboriously and wonders how best to say 'I did not come up with an idea until asked'. But, hold on. It is hard to read between the lines from this distance. Auer may well have been popular. In 1841, at the age of twenty-five, he took on a failing company with forty-five employees and within a decade, as a direct result of his industry and ambition, it had become a 'major state polygraphic institute' with a staff of over nine hundred. Moreover, it occupied a position close to the intellectual heart of Europe. And throughout Auer's term, the remit of the Imperial State Printing-Office was one of enlightenment based on the dissemination of information and education. The factory in Singerstraße became a tourist destination itemised in Baedeker, where one might see

a rare combination, and in such perfection, of the entire range of all branches of graphic representation, printing, type foundry, stereotype printing, copperplate and lithography, nature-print, photography, galvanography.

Andrew Worring might have wanted to give a little credit to the man who had worked so hard to secure his future, and who was so very enthusiastic about his quite simple idea.

The London Print Studio (Round Two)

Pia faces the plate-glass window that contains a reflection of the All Stars Boxing Gym and Youth Club. Seconds out for Round Two at the London Print Studio. The sunshine on the canal makes the studio dazzlingly bright. It's how things are, today. See the light dance on the ceiling. Like a big fish-tank. She has booked the Rochat 32" etching press for two reasons: in the first place, the results from Gosport and Dagenham suggest an intaglio press is likely to succeed. Secondly, she is armed with fresh advice from Michael Twyman who, in a letter, has also invited her to Reading. (This may be why the sun is shining.)

The press is not old but it looks ancient, the printing equivalent of a penny farthing with its outsize handwheel and cast-iron frame. The engineering firm of Harry F Rochat still makes these machines and has worldwide sales. She has used a press like this before and is soon underway, carding warm sepia ink across the plate in two directions then wiping off the surface with new tarlatan scrims. She lays slightly dampened paper over the plate on the bed of the press, and then the blankets. Turning the wheel, she imagines the soft felt pushing the paper into the fine inked lines on the plate with text-book precision; so when she folds back the blankets, holds up the paper and contemplates the patchy result, there is a sense of disappointment even though she knows it takes time to resolve the variables – to adjust the pressure, to get the ink to the right consistency and so on.

'Pleased?' asks the technician who happens to be passing by.

'Not really,' she says, with a smile.

'I'll be back,' he says, as he leaves the room.

Further efforts show some improvement. Just not much. She notices a certain tarnish from the lead, a halo effect around the image that gives it an antique quality. Under different circumstances this would appeal to her. The ghostly aura that emanates from these prints lends them a melancholy aspect, as if the past is leaking out at the edges. Marvellous, except that what she wants is a clean image. Pia leaves the building and once again heads for the Wedlake Street Foot-bridge to watch ducks dabbling about on the canal. On her return the technician is hovering nearby. After making a couple of prints, he diagnoses insufficient pressure and is confident that he has the answer.

'Let's add blankets.'

She nods. That had also occurred to her. 'But I'm afraid that I'll flatten the plate.'

The technician smiles indulgently. 'You won't.'

'It's lead. It's very soft.'

'It'll be fine.'

Blankets are added and the result is less than fine. The gingko plate emerges from the press twice as long and half as thick. Ripples of felt obscure the leaf's dichotomous venation. It is crushed and so, it seems, is the technician. Crestfallen, he remembers there is some-where he needs to be and leaves her to ponder the power of this press. Could she use it to make plates? In her bag are two small tiles of lead and sections of dried fern frond. She sandwiches a section of Hard fern between one of these pieces of lead and a steel plate, reduces the number of blankets and turns the press. In no time she has two dazzling new plates and but for the gingko fiasco she would not have even made the attempt. Making prints does not prove any easier: on the first copy the outline is sharp but the image way too dark and there is no detail. Try again: scuffing across the image – well, that's no surprise, given the rough surface. Once again: half of the image is missing, though on the other half it is good. On the next the halo-effect is stronger than usual and there is distortion. And on another there is a level of fine detail but also some splodges and no ink at all on parts of the stem. In this way the afternoon passes and by the close she has a stack of smudged and smeary work to review. The prints from the new plates may be as imperfect as those made in the morning. It's hard to view the work objectively and from a distance it seems quite good. Look more closely and it's clear any judgement of the day rests on a split decision: she can make plates but is unable to print from them.

The delicate pamphlet that Pia came across in the National Art Library, in which Auer gives himself plenty of credit for 'the discovery of the natural-printing process', was published in April 1853, in several languages. A small work and yet much space is dedicated to the filing of patent 7698 in relation to the process (in October, 1852) and more importantly, to the resolution that it should be 'given up for general benefit' (in April, 1853). Auer makes a point of explaining:

> I paid out of my own property the increased expenses, in order to prepare not only in time the possibility of giving up the possession of the patent, but also to prevent the taking out of a patent in any state of a foreign country, and thus to ensure to custom not only the honour of the discovery, but also a proof of its disinterestedness.

What is this all about? Ask Bradbury, maybe he knows, because there have been all kinds of rumours since his return to London early in 1853. Some say he left Vienna under a cloud, others say he is up to something. He will tell you it is no big deal, that he had a good time on his travels and that the State Printing-office, by the way, is very impressive.

There is a good chance he might omit to mention that members of the family firm, William Bradbury and Frederick Mullett Evans, have applied for a patent of their own (No. 1164, dated May 11, sealed June 28 and filed in the Great Seal Patent Office on November 11, 1853) for 'Improvements in taking impressions and producing printing surfaces'. A copper-plate is provided in support of the application, the very one that Bradbury was given as a keepsake on his departure from Vienna. Eventually Bradbury comes clean, in his own way, with a presentation to the Society of Arts; and shortly after, he writes to Auer:

Sir, I have the honour to address you upon the Printing Process 'Naturselbstdruck' which you in conjunction with Andrew Worrung [sic], factor of the Galvanoplastic Department, claim as Inventor and Introducer – I wish now to acquaint you with the fact that England took the priority in Establishing the process of the Naturselbstdruck, in the name and person of Ferguson Branson, MD Cantab., who read a paper, and produced printed specimens, before the Society of Arts, John Street, Adelphi London, in the year 1847 March 19th and 26th, and that at Birmingham in 1848 he made the first proofs.

You must now understand that neither yourself nor Andrew Worrung [sic] (much as I value his practical knowledge) can claim the originality of the Naturselbstdruck (or as I have named it Phytoglyphy) and that England – and not Austria – has furnished a worthy pendant to the Galvanoplastic of Jacobi of Russia and the Daguerreotype of Daguerre of France.

You must be aware through Mr Paul Pretsch, that Bradbury and Evans have patented – not the Invention – but Improvements upon the original Invention.

I went to the Society of Arts today and the Secretary pointed this out to me upon my examining specimens you had so graciously sent to that Society. An Englishman also claims the Invention – 14 years ago – the Invention of Galvanography –

If it should meet with your views from time to time we will exchange specimens of the Naturselbstdruck of Austria and England and make a mutual progress together. Awaiting your reply I remain Yours very truly, Henry Bradbury.

This is a declaration of hostilities in which Auer's most sententious phrases, his 'worthy pendants' are thrown in his face. No wonder Auer believes the letter to be 'deprived of every epistolary etiquette'.

One more thing. Bradbury also sends a gift, a print made from Auer's keepsake. At the foot of the print is a line of text:

Bradbury & Evans, Patentees, Whitefriars.

On Google Maps it looked an easy stroll to the university but this turns out to be a serious miscalculation, a problem intensified by the rain that has just started to fall with purpose. Judging from the way the small wheels on her suitcase wobble and groan alarmingly, it must seem as if Pia is visiting for a month. The case contains her work to-date, plus spare plates of lead. The road is long and progress is slow, an allegory of her nature-printing life. She loses her way in the campus parkland, heads cross-country towards woodland and stumbles on Black Bridge, one of two routes across a narrow strip of ornamental lake. Out of breath and in less than perfect humour she is late for her appointment at the Department of Typography and Graphic Communication.

Martin Andrews, a tall white-haired man, takes her on a tour of the low-roofed barracks-style building. Here are various immaculate workspaces, planning chests and type cabinets, all perfectly arranged and compartmentalised. None is being used. On the walls are old enamel signs, posters with detailed information on printing techniques, an exhibition about a typographer called Berthold Wolpe. Here is a library and there, the offices of the Ephemera Society. They walk through Letterpress into the Lithography and Intaglio bay where she comes upon an old friend, a Harry Rochat rolling press.

'We used to have a lot of presses here. They have been in storage since the graphics industry switched over to computers.'

There is a tinge of regret in Martin's voice. Like Michael Twyman he studied here, then became a lecturer. Retired now, he returns regularly to teach certain courses. Pia wonders aloud why Reading has become a centre for historical research of printing, when the art departments of most academic establishments pay lip service to letterpress and crafts such as linocutting, wood-engraving and etching. The responsibility may lie with Robert

Gibbings, who taught both men. Perhaps best-known as the author of *Sweet Thames Run Softly*, a pastoral idyll published during the Second World War, Gibbings was responsible for a revival in wood engraving and he founded the Society of Wood Engravers. The Golden Cockerel press under his auspices became the finest of all the private presses. He was a public figure, an artist, an adventurous traveller, a writer, naturalist and naturist; and he was also, in euphemistic phrase, larger-than-life.

One other notable personality is associated with the place. William Henry Fox Talbot established a studio work-shop in Reading to prepare the large number of salt prints produced as tip-ins for *The Pencil of Nature*, the first commercial book to be illustrated with photographs that was released in facsicles between 1844 and 1846. (A limited edition with hand-written text of Anna Atkins' beautiful *Photographs of British Algae, Cyanotype Impressions* had been self-published eight months earlier, in October 1843.)

In Michael Twyman's office the conversation turns slowly towards nature-printing. Like Michael, Martin knows the work of Auer and Bradbury but he has not taken an active interest. After all it is just one of many short-lived novelties that appeared in Victorian times, when all kinds of amateurs aspired to being inventors; even in disciplines about which they knew very little, including printing.

'For example,' says Martin, 'have you heard about wire-plate engraving?' This comprised a printing block made from a bunch of wire rods, like a packet of uncooked spaghetti on its end. An image in relief was supposed to be made by pushing some rods down, printing from those that remained raised. It was published as a serious proposal, but did not go beyond the conceptual stage. Pia wonders whether nature-printing is held to be a similarly eccentric episode in the history of print. Michael and Martin study the prints that she has made. They acknowledge the difficulties and defects and are generous in their praise. Martin is interested in the plates and his eyes light up when she offers to demonstrate the technique. They head directly for the Rochat press where she performs her usual trick, this time with an oak leaf. The audience knows what is supposed to happen and, as in the best magic, everything is in plain sight. The lead plate is duly produced, an 'Andrew Worring' moment that generates warm appreciation.

'It's hard, though, to print from material as soft as lead,' says Martin.

'There are alternatives,' Michael murmurs, as he tilts the plate to the light. 'When we met, I could see you were keen. I wasn't sure you'd persevere.' He looks at her. 'What are your plans?'

She isn't fully prepared for this question. The quick answer is that she'd like to learn how to make plates like Bradbury, or like Auer and his team. At a deeper level is a sense that she might be able to recover something that got lost in the headlong rush for profit through progress. The way she sees it, nature-printing was conceived as a method of obtaining an accurate representation of an object at low cost for mass-market publishing. Unable to meet any of these criteria, it was simply abandoned. But from her perspective commercial and theoretical failings are unimportant. All she wants to do (say it again) is make a few prints as good as those in Bradbury's book. For her, nature-printing provides an opportunity to make a beautiful image.

Michael tells her that she would benefit from access to the specialist library. He extends to her the opportunity to work at Reading on an informal basis. Later, when she tells a friend about this outcome, he is incredulous.

'These days,' he says, 'when universities are considered to be businesses, any proposal focused on the encouragement of learning sounds implausible.'

Membership of organisations is sometimes a way to meet like-minded individuals. Sometimes it serves as a means of gaining access to facilities, or status. Usually it offers a sense of belonging and this is what Pia needs, plus the chance to put her research in context. The connection between ferns and nature-printing is firmly established in her mind and it is worth joining the Fern Society (strictly the British Pteridological Society, or BPS) for the membership pack alone: sticker, leather bookmark, a magazine, plus a book-sized annual bulletin. It is like a throwback to childhood clubs joined on the promise of material benefits. The society organises field trips too and this is why, towards the end of the summer, she is on her way to Rickmansworth, inching through heavy traffic on the motorway in her friend's battered Ford.

'Ferns appeared at least 333 million years before we began to swing through the trees,' says Caroline, just making conversation. 'Of course, we got held-up on the M25.'

The small group assembled in a car-park at the edge of Bishop's wood is at pains to assure them that they are not late but sets off immediately along woodland paths under blue skies. 'You know you are among botanists,' whispers Caroline, 'when everyone wears their trousers tucked in their socks.' She is no exception and explains that it is a way to counter the threat of infection from ticks, tiny arachnids that can carry Lyme disease. While Pia stoops to look the part, Caroline sets off in deep discussion with an old friend about the defining characteristics of ancient woodland in Hertfordshire. The features vary across the country according to the prevailing conditions – here, the blend of gravelly soils and London Clay have produced an exceptionally rich woodland. Later Pia discovers that with a local group in Surrey Caroline is trying to protect a tract of land from development by proving it should be awarded 'ancient woodland' status. The prospective builders are making things awkward by denying access. How strange it is, that a few individuals or members of seemingly insignificant amateur bodies are all that stands between our landscape and the endless expansion of housing estates and golf-courses. These trouser-in-socks botanists are engaged in serious work, maintaining records of distribution, monitoring the ecology of the country, standing up to big money's slick legal teams; and allowing us to consider what we stand to lose, or have lost already.

Pia explains that she a beginner and gets encouraging murmurs in reply. 'If you see anything remotely fern-like, give a shout,' says Tim, the tall man strolling alongside. They are soon among them. Is this Golden scaly male fern (*Dryopteris affinis*) or Borrer's scaly male fern (*Dryopteris borreri*)? Here is Common male fern (*Dryopteris filix-mas*) which doesn't look very different from either of the others. Growing conveniently side by side are examples of Broad buckler fern (*Dryopteris dilatata*) and Narrow buckler fern (*Dryopteris carthusiana*) and Tim takes the trouble to point out the differences. Here the stipe (stalk) is dark green. There it is light green. Look at the scales. These are striped. Those are plain. Ah, yes! Once there's an explanation, it is exciting to register a positive identification. Pia takes Tim's advice and draws the group's attention to a stand of ferns that has gone unnoticed. 'Ah yes, *Pteridium aquilinum*,' says Howard, the expedition leader. 'Always good to see.' He doesn't sound entirely genuine and the group moves on. Pia wonders if they don't like novices seeing things that they have failed to notice. 'That's Bracken,' hisses Caroline. 'It's a pest.' It's also everywhere.

Over lunch it emerges that there is an ulterior motive behind Pia's interest in ferns. There is an unexpected level of knowledge of, and enthusiasm for, nature-printing. One or two people in the society have researched the subject thoroughly, they all know Thomas Moore's work, and Tim explains that *The Ferns of Great Britain and Ireland* is a holy grail for collectors. He owns two framed prints from a broken copy of the folio edition. There is general agreement that Bradbury's images of ferns are among the finest ever made. If it proves possible to make nature-prints in the same way, then members of the BPS, at least, will want to know.

In the afternoon they visit a sub-tropical garden in west London. Northwood Hills is roughly the same vintage as Becontree in Dagenham on the opposite side of the capital, but the charms of these homes were marketed to the genteel classes in terms of bucolic balderdash that should make estate agents blush:

> Each lover of Metroland may well have his own wood beech and
> coppice – all tremulous green loveliness in Spring and russet
> gold in October.

They are soon in a semi-detached privet-free street (Ferndown!) of bricked- and paved-over gardens. In such an environment David Bryson's place, with its giant fronds beckoning gently, is easy to find. An astonishing garden with palms, cycads, cacti, aloes, bamboos, bananas, cordylines, creepers draped over trees – and ferns, the majority of which are aliens, like the giant Blechnums and specimens of *Dicksonia antarctica* Pia recognises from the Physic Garden fernery. The garden contains rarities including *Trichycarpus princeps*, a palm discovered only twenty years ago on sheer stone cliffs in the Yunnan province of South Central China. The strangeness of finding it here, trembling in the rumble of carriages from the Metropolitan line just beyond the bottom of the garden.

Paul Pretsch (like Walter Woodbury) is another of those bit-part players whose life throws an oblique light on the history of nature-printing. It is curious that Bradbury should mention Pretsch, senior manager at the printing-office, in his provocative letter to Auer. Bradbury may have studied under Pretsch during his time at Vienna. They would have met at the Great Exhibition where Pretsch organised the Austrian stand and among other things took at least ten of the highly regarded photographs shown there. He accepted a Prize medal under his own name for photography and also the Council medal awarded to the Imperial Court and Government Printing-office of Vienna:

> for their new process in typography, galvanoplastic, and chemitypic printing; for the variety of the Oriental types, and perfect execution of the punches, as well as for the general excellence of the numerous specimens exhibited in stereotyping, electrotyping, printing and bookbinding.

That Pretsch is given due credit for his work was the cause of unnecessary awkwardness. Andrew Worring could have explained that employees of the Staatsdruckerei were obliged to credit *all* productions of the printing-office to its director. Pretsch, who like Auer had trained as a typesetter, saw things differently. He joined the printing-office less than a year after Auer and established levels of expertise in several departments. He saw no need to defer to Auer, but the outcome was never in doubt. Auer may have underrated photography but it remained an operation for which he was ultimately responsible.

Shortly after Bradbury's letter to Auer, Pretsch invented a new method of printing photographs and rather than surrender it to the greater good he gave up his comfortable position, moved to London and patented the process under his own name in Britain (Patent 2,373) and later, in Austria.

At this time, photography is still in its infancy. The job of taking a photograph is painstaking, requires a chemist's expertise. Making any kind of copy is equally tedious. The possibilities of the medium are in doubt. Auer prefers nature-printing, which:

> delivers without human intervention everything that a thinking being could want from a copied depiction.

In comparison, the 'light-print' has a number of disadvantages. Prints tend to require significant retouching, which undermines their objectivity. They fade over time. Auer also dislikes what he calls photography's 'armed eye', its ability to make images from afar. To his mind, the physical distance between subject and camera is a disadvantage in comparison with the full-on contact required for nature-printing – its direct rendering of the visual and textural qualities of the same object. These days, when there is complete familiarity with the gap between camera and subject, image and reality, it seems a peculiar objection. Lastly Auer knows it is impossible to print photographs on any press, which limits their usefulness. This is why 'on account of its simplicity [nature-printing] is of more importance than the printing by light and the galvanoplastic'.

Pretsch is one of the pioneers of photography and his big idea – photo-galvanography – has a suitably intimidating name. As a way of printing photographs it is nearly brilliant and it remains an important milestone on the road which leads, about thirty years later, to the half-tone process that secures the future of photography. His newly formed Photo-Galvanographic Company takes premises on the Holloway Road and over the next couple of years produces decent work in a serial portfolio called *Photographic Art Treasures*. Pretsch's associate is the distinguished photographer Roger Fenton[1], a founder and first secretary of the Photographic Society of London. The company is never a success. It proves difficult and time-consuming to achieve results with the correct tonal range. Most plates have to be retouched extensively. How Pretsch must have wished for the resources of the old firm, or for its commercial immunity. It doesn't help that Campbell Duncan Dallas, a former manager of Pretsch's business, sets up in direct competition offering 'Dallastypes'. Dallas's claims to the invention are given short shrift by experts from various countries. The more serious problem for Pretsch is William Henry Fox Talbot, a wealthy and litigious man with influential contacts who believes Pretsch has infringed his patented use of bichromated gelatine. This is bad news for Pretsch because Talbot is prepared to go to great lengths to enforce a patent. While their prepared plates are materially the same, the photo-galvanographic process delivers very different results. Talbot is quite impressed, though he notes 'my object has been to render the Art quite independent of the Engraver...to do the whole by natural processes'. Once again the inference is that work requiring intervention is inferior. Pretsch is aware of the problem and includes the phrase 'absolutely untouched' in captions by photo-galvanographic images shown at later exhibitions. Such efforts are futile since his enterprise languishes in a Sargasso of solicitors for several years. Pretsch pleads with Talbot:

Some years of thought and anxiety I have devoted to the purpose of making photography subject to the press... the result of my exercises has not been a failure, but it has been purposely made a failure.

1 Fenton's images of the conflict in the Crimea make him one of the world's first war photographers. An exhibition of more than three hundred of these images toured the country. He also supplied pictures for Henry Bradbury's book, *Printing, Its Dawn, Day and Destiny*.

Sympathy is not forthcoming so Pretsch attempted a different tack by proposing a partnership. He tried to ingratiate himself by recommending the services of a company for acierage – Bradbury, Wilkinson & Co. Pretsch even offers to buy a licence from Talbot, but the terms are too severe. In his penultimate rather pathetic letter to Talbot, Pretsch says:

> Since several years I have been living on my own resources… which are now perfectly exhausted, and at an end without any hope of being renewed. I do not suppose that it is your intention, to torture me; – I think I have not deserved such degrading pains for my hard labour and unceasing skillfull [sic] work.

By this time the Photo-Galvanographic Company has collapsed. Pretsch is bankrupt. His patent, allowed to lapse. A public appeal is launched to assist him. For a while he works for De la Rue as an engraver; in the end he returns to Vienna in ill-health and accepts a job at, of all places, the Imperial Printing-office.

The Type 5 protective body suit arrives by post, a fetching onesie with a drawstring hood. In the yard behind the flat, using a drill with a sanding disc, Pia polishes sheets of ordinary roofing lead. A friend from Sweden takes a picture of her – kneeling over a plate in full kit, complete with mask, goggles and gloves – and it reaches her parents. One evening their neighbours come over for dinner and when the conversation turns to children 'Pia's Project' is outlined with some humour, some exaggeration, and with the image of their daughter dressed as a forensic investigator at a crime scene. The neighbours are horrified. Mother and Father look again at the picture and next morning she receives the first 'anxious parents' phonecall for years.

Working with lead *is* difficult. As the directors of LeadAtom predicted, transportation of the polished plates is a nuisance; a single plate loses its shape when another is placed on it. It proves necessary to hold her adapted box file (containing two lead plates) in both hands like a tray, as close to the horizontal as possible; as if she is the custodian of something fragile, or possibly dangerous. Thus her procession through Paddington station is best described as stately. The journey is a drag but Pia settles easily at Reading, turns up regularly once or twice a week and picks up tips such as bevelling the corners of the plate to prevent them digging in the paper. A polished plate is also an improvement – easier to ink and to wipe clean, with slightly less staining of the paper – but the lead continues to tarnish. As soon as ink is applied, the shiniest of surfaces clouds over. One friend suggests using varnish to counter the tarnishing, but this doesn't work. The varnish fails to adhere to the surface. Further coats make a small difference but are soon rubbed off by the white spirit that must be used to clean the plate. A scientist at the Physic Garden lends her an indecipherable pamphlet on the structure of inks. Another friend who works in art conservation suggests an ascorbic acid-based cleansing agent. This doesn't make any difference either. Tarnation.

Martin is quick to make suggestions. He wants her to experiment, which she is happy to do – though her sights remain, as ever, fixed on nature-printing. One day he demonstrates in a matter of minutes how to create an image similar to one of Bradbury's prints, using a softground technique. A maple leaf is laid on a prepared aluminium plate and run through the intaglio press. Non-image areas are painted with stop-out and when the ground has been hardened the plate is etched with what Martin calls 'a non-toxic mordant'. The results are impressive, but lack the distinct relief of nature-prints. It would be easy to head in a different direction. There are many possible paths. Setbacks, small gains, nagging doubts. The quality of the images in Bradbury's book and the impressive work that emerged from Vienna help to keep her focused.

* * *

The softground demo and the throwaway remark about short-lived novelties jostle the confidence and it feels important suddenly to put nature-printing in context. Printing today is, for the most part, a straightforward industry. Printers in each sector modify their presses – or more often their binding lines and finishing options – to gain competitive advantages, but it is possible to count the basic processes on the fingers of one hand. Easy to assume things were equally simple in the Nineteenth Century, when letterpress dominated the printing of text and the basic design of most presses would not have fazed Gutenberg; except that, when it comes to images, the picture is not clear at all.

At the Department of Prints and Drawings in the British Museum is a book called *The Art Exemplar* by William J Stannard, subtitled *A Guide to Distinguish One Species of Print From Another With Pictorial Examples And Written Descriptions of Every Known Style.*

It is Stannard's own copy. On a pasted-in slip is a hand-written comment:

> Note. There are only three other Copies of the Work this size:—
> namely those possessed by
> H.M. The Queen
> Earl Ellesmere
> The Lord Chief Baron Kelly
> Six additional copies on small paper completed the number
> published. Harry Sandars.

According to Elizabeth Harris, Harry Sandars *is* Stannard. The edition is limited because the 'pictorial examples' were taken from Stannard's own collection of prints. For this reason there are differences between copies. The contents listed on the exotic title page reveal the extent of developments and it is impossible to resist giving the details. Those with a limited interest in Victorian printing processes should leap-frog the rest of this paragraph. Stannard's indiscriminate catalogue includes: Acrography, Alto-relievo, Amphytype, Anaglyptography, Anastic, Anthotype, Aquatint, Autography, Bank-note printing, Bates's process, Baxter's process, Baxterotype, Becker's patent, Block printing, Book printing, Calotype, Camieux engraving, Cast engraving, Catalysotype, Chalcography, Chalcoxylography, Chalk style, Chemitypy, Chiaru-scuro, Chromolithography, Chromotype, Chromotypography, Chrono-lithography, Chrysotype, Clichée pierres, Collas's process, Color printing, Compound-plate printing, Copper plate engraving, Cribble, Curvilinear printing, Cyanotype, Daguerreotype, Dotting engraving, Drawing style, Durertype, Electric printing, Electro printing, Electro surface printing, Electro-magnetic engraving, Electrography, Electrotint, Electrotype, Elliottype, Encreux engraving, Endotting, Energiatype, Engraved drawing, Engraving, Engraving in stereotype, Etching, Fern printing, Ferrotype, Galvanic

Etching, Galvanoglyphy, Galvanography, Galvanoplastic, Galvanotype, Geometric engraving, Glyphography, Heliobyssotype, Heliochromy, Heliography, Helioplastic, Hillotype, Identigraphy, Illuminated printing, Killasography, Lavis-lithography, Letter-press printing, Lignograph, Line engraving, Litho-photography, Lithochromy, Lithography, Lithotint, Lithozographia, Logography, Logotype, Machinagraphy, Medallion engraving, Metageltine process, Metallic relief engraving, Metalography, Mezzotint, Micro-photography, Mikrotypopurogenelion, Mineralography, Mixed style, Nature printing, Niello, Niellography, Oil printing, Oleocaleography, Omnygraphy, Omotype, Opus Mallei, Paleography, Paneiconography, Papyrography, Photo-Flemish process, Photo-lithography, Photo-metallography, Photogalvanography, Photogenic printing, Photography, Photoxylography, Phytoglyphy, Poikilography, Poliplasiasmos, Polychromatype, Polyautography, Polygraphy, Polytypography, Quadrelography, Rose-engine engraving, Rubbing style, Siderographia, Single line engraving, Soft etching, Statue engraving, Steel engraving, Steel letter press engraving, Stereo-glyphography, Stereotypography, Stipple engraving, Stokes's patent, Stump style, Stylography, Surface printing, Taille douce, Talbotype, Thermography, Tinted lithography, Tinted xylographs, Tissierography, Tornography, Transferooraphy, Typi-fixi, Typi-mobile, Typography, Typometry, Via sicca process, Vitro-heliography, Voltaic engraving, Wood engraving, Word printing, Xylography, Yuftsotype, Zincography.

The suffixes 'typy' and 'graphy' take a pounding and you would need 'the dead dictionary' (Stannard's words) to make sense of some of these names. Many, as Harris points out, refer to the same thing (eg, Fern Printing, Nature-Printing, Phytoglyphy) and by stripping out these and other secondary graphic procedures (eg, typography) the number of different processes falls to 'about forty'. All the same. To discover such a bewildering array of ideas with hubristic titles and (mostly) brief lives, now utterly lost, is a sobering moment. And as Stannard points out these are just the ones that saw action. There were many more ('their name is legion') that were proposed but never pursued in practice. Wire-plate engraving comes to mind. The maelstrom of progress over printing at this time makes Pia's decision to pursue nature-printing seem whimsical until she turns a page in Stannard and is suddenly face-to-face with an astonishingly beautiful image of *'Epilobrium augustifolium'* (Rosebay Willowherb) printed by Bradbury and Evans, Whitefriars, London. Nothing else in the book comes close. The freshness and delicacy of the printed plant has outlasted its name (now *Chamerion augustifolia*).

With her usual tact Harris states that Stannard's account of nature-printing is 'quite objective' and the qualification is necessary, for it seems the entry owes much to the influence of Bradbury. Alongside an unnecessary and severe discrediting of Auer, who has 'claimed a far larger share of this interesting process than he merits', is the indication that Bradbury's patented method is 'in many particulars a material improvement upon...that in use in Vienna'. This is an exaggeration – in fact, as far as Pia can work out, it is exactly the same.

Following the fern-hunt in Metroland rumours of Pia's nature-printing project have reached Adrian Dyer, a retired botanist and self-taught pteridologist whose own interest in nature-printing was sparked by the discovery in 1959 of a copy of Moore's book of ferns in the basement of Blackwell's, complete with fifty-one folio prints by Henry Bradbury. Since then, Adrian has pieced together fragments of Bradbury's life and more than fifty years on probably knows as much as anyone about the man. He is in the course of assembling his accumulated knowledge of Bradbury in a biography and sends a draft to be 'Pia-reviewed'. In return, she is happy to share her findings of the printing process.

The manuscript turns out to be a thorough piece of research covering the life and works of Henry Bradbury. Passages from *Autotypography*, an extremely rare book written by Bradbury shortly before his death, are included. (The copy in the British Library was destroyed during the War.) Pia's secret hope, that this might turn out to be a manual for nature-printers, is soon dashed. There is little beyond assertive and defensive arguments relating to the discovery and she still flinches from that debate. A person's reputation can impinge on the value of the work. For the moment her focus remains on Bradbury's printing rather than on details of his family, the places he lived, the circumstances of his death.

She asks Adrian what he thinks about Bradbury's 'material improvement' to Auer's process. In the context of patent applications Adrian accepts the word 'improvement' is generic rather than meaningful and there is no clue to its significance in anything written by Bradbury. Nevertheless he believes that Bradbury may have facilitated the operation of cutting and polishing lead plates by deploying an innovative Planing Machine developed by J & RM Wood, a firm of printers' engineers. It may be so. Her knowledge of Viennese lead-polishing methods is sketchy. Regrettably Wood's machine is no longer available, for it certainly sounds better than a hand-drill and a body suit.

Bradbury continues to wind-up Auer through the pages of *The Atheneum*. An undated and unattributed clipping from that journal (pasted in the V&A's copy of a Bradbury book) serves as one such example:

> M. Auer complains that Mr Henry Bradbury has carried away from Vienna the secrets of the imperial printing office, and has published these as his own, in England, without right. This is a question to be discussed on the facts; but M. Auer has chosen to discuss it otherwise, imputing into his dispute, with abominable taste, personal concerns and personal scandals, which, whether true or false, have no relation to the issues sought by the writer.

This is defensive jingoism: any murmurs from Vienna about Bradbury's behaviour prove the foreigner Auer is a cad and a bounder. The article develops what became Bradbury's stock position in respect of nature-printing, viz that it is not a recent invention, that it has been around for centuries, that it has little to do with Vienna; and it finishes with a humdinger:

> Had he [Bradbury] taken out a patent he would have exercised a legal right without violating any moral obligation. But it appears he refrained – leaving the art open to every one with skill and patience to prove it.

As Auer knows, Bradbury applied for a patent practically as soon as his feet were back on dry ground after his European tour. There is no evidence he allowed anyone else to enter the field.

A little later in December 1853, Auer's process is described in *The Atheneum*. This article also mentions Bradbury's intentions to publish his own work, then throws open to question whether Vienna is correct to claim the invention given that Birmingham has for some time been working in the same way. In the very next issue WC Aitken (of Birmingham) announces that he came up with the very same idea 'about twelve months ago'. Which is tricky, since this timing would not give him priority over the Staatsdruckerei. (No-one entertains the possibility that, this being the case, Aitken might have lifted the idea from Vienna.) Bradbury deals with the problem by suggesting, in a footnote to Aitken's letter, that credit for the invention can be given to another Englishman:

...for in the year 1851, in March, Mr Ferguson Branson not only read before the Society of Arts a report of a process, identically the same as that claimed by the Austrian patentees, but even produced printed specimens to illustrate more fully the true meaning of the inventions'.

It is possible *The Atheneum* realises it is being used to stir things up. On December 17 it issues an endnote:

Natural Printing – On this subject we have received letters from Mr Aitken and Dr Branson. We cannot enter into the question here raised of priority of claim – and to print the letters would involve us in a controversy to which we see no end, and of which we question the utility.

A few months later Auer publishes an unambiguous disquisition, *The Conduct of a Young Englishman named Henry Bradbury at the Imperial and Government Printing-office in Vienna, and after his return to his native-country, in opposition to the acknowledgments of the foreign countries concerning the NATURAL-PRINTING-PROCESS invented by Alois Auer, government counsellor, and Andrew Worring, manager. The conduct of Bradbury ascertained by all the members of the Imperial Printing-office with more than 700 signatures.* The work is published simultaneously in German, Italian, French and English. Auer accuses Bradbury of spreading 'fictitious notices…destitute of truth, for the English newspapers'. It is said that while in Vienna, Bradbury asked Auer for money, he 'contracted debts', and that he attempted to 'bribe the overseer by the offer of 40 fl for the purpose of obtaining a more perfect set of specimens for his dishonest designs'. An attempt which, according to Auer, was reported immediately. (Auer states later, in *Mein Dienstleben*, that a supervisor did betray the secrets of the Printing-office to Bradbury.) Do many people care? It is hard to understand why a man in Auer's position should have become quite so worked-up over a disappointing young guest. Let's restore a sense of perspective. As nefarious activities go it's small beer – though in view of further charges against Bradbury this may be an unfortunate choice of expression:

> he visited the printing-office of Messrs Gottlieb Haase and Sons, whereupon he triumphantly related in an inn – perhaps intoxicated, as he often happened to be during his stay in Vienna – how he had deceived the Imperial Printing-office, and bribed the overseers, and how much he was astonished, that foreigners like him, were freely admitted to acquire so perfect a knowledge of the various artistical branches practised there!

This has a ring of truth and is clearly bad form, though the inclusion of snide asides on Bradbury's drinking habits also seems lacking in taste.

Walking among the Order beds early one morning before the Garden opens, searching for leaves to press, Pia notices the Education Officer is striding purposefully in her direction. Might a nature-printing course be pencilled in for the following year? It feels like a terrifying prospect, but it should be possible to make monoprints. A box is ticked and Pia returns to the beds. It is difficult to find fit subjects to work with in October. The plants are wilting and a cool breeze sends shrivelled leaves scurrying away across the grass.

Later that evening she receives a call from California, a response to a letter written to the Nature-Printing Society asking if anyone knew anything about Bradbury's style of printing. Eric Hochberg, founder-member of the Nature-Printing Society, is following things up. They discuss Peter Heilmann and she learns he has been unwell. She outlines her progress and touches on the problem of tarnishing. Unfortunately Eric isn't aware of anyone working in this area, but he does remember seeing Auer's plates in Vienna. This is such big news Pia isn't sure if she has heard correctly.

'Sure,' says Eric, who can sense her excitement from Santa Barbara. 'But I really can't remember exactly where – it was 1987. I was still working as a marine biologist and I was on my way somewhere else. Perhaps it was in the Botany department at the university.'

Only two plates are known, according to Cave – one in Harvard and the other in the Enschedé museum at Haarlem. To discover others would be special and Pia knows that sight of them would inform her own work although, if they do exist, they are unlikely to be made of lead. She rushes to compose an email to the University of Vienna. Receiving no reply, Pia chooses a different name from the contact list and pushes another email into the dark. Weeks pass before a response to the first arrives, apologising for the delay, citing mail server issues.

An anonymous administrator explains that there is no trace of any of Auer's plates in the library's collections; that, so far as they are aware, none of the plates from the state printing-house survives; and that the printing-house, now a private concern, has confirmed it does not hold any plates either. Pia is thanked for her interest.

She is still sifting this disappointment when an email from Vienna drops in her Inbox from Robert Stangl, her second-choice recipient. He apologises for the delay, referencing the same server problems. And then he tells her that the library *does* own plates. They are stored at the Faculty Centre of Biodiversity, part of the Natural History Museum. She is welcome to make an appointment. It seems an extraordinary piece of luck. Had she received a prompt response to her first email, there would have been no reason to pursue the matter any further. By electronic sleight of hand, the plates have materialised. It feels important to get to Vienna before they disappear again.

* * *

Most writers on the subject agree that while lead is perfect for taking an impression it is too soft to be of much use as a printing plate. Pia has not found this to be exactly the case. While it is possible to make up to twelve prints from a plate without any loss of detail, the problem is there appears no easy answer to the question of oxidisation – a reaction accelerated by inks, white spirit, or water – that makes the non-image areas of the page grubby. Lead is vulnerable to scratches and it is weak under pressure. Printing is by definition a method of obtaining repeatable results and for Auer, the lead impression was only an intermediate step. At the beginning of *Discovery of the Natural Printing-Process*, he explains:

If a greater number of copies are required, which the lead-form on account of its softness is not capable of furnishing, it is stereotyped in the case of being printed at typographical press, or galvanised in the case of being worked at copper-plate press, as many times as necessary, and the impressions are taken from the stereotyped or galvanised plate instead of from the lead-plate.

Research has brought her to the point where she understands this means that a hard copper-plate is made from the soft lead original by a technique known variously as stereotyping, galvanisation, or electrotyping. To someone without knowledge of chemistry it sounds intimidating. Perhaps she can take heart from the advice given in the *Polytechnic Journal* of 1843:

The (electrotype) process is as suitable for ladies to practise in their drawing-rooms as any of their usual amusements.

O, for the dauntless ingenuity of Victorians. Pia is unwilling to tackle 19th Century science and this is why a chance remark by Michael Twyman to the effect that he thought some nature-printing plates were made from pewter strikes her with the force of an opportunity, even though she does not know quite what pewter is and cannot recall reading about pewter in conjunction with nature-printing.

Pewter is a flowery English word for tin mixed with other metals – known only as tin in Germany (zinn) and France (étain). The ingredients and their exact proportions have varied over time and according to end-use. A contemporary source, *Tomlinson's Cyclopedia* published in 1854, suggests 'Common Pewter' is 'an alloy of about 80 parts of tin and 20 of lead; but other metals such as copper, antimony and zinc, are sometimes added'. English pewter today, naturally, is made without lead. Records of a guild of pewterers date back to 1348. The Worshipful Company of Pewterers was granted a royal charter in 1474 and shortly afterwards awarded powers to regulate the trade[1]. According to the Worshipful Company's website:

> The prosperity of the trade may be said to have reached its zenith in the late Seventeenth Century. Thereafter, partly because society's drinking habits changed following the introduction of tea to this country and partly because the

---

1 Regulation came about because in Henry VIII's time there was a brain-drain of pewterers who 'for their singular Lucre, repaired into Strange Regions and Countries', allegedly resulting in an influx of cheap 'Pewter untruly mixed' that threatened to undermine the craft of pewterers 'which at this day setteth and keepeth in Work and Occupation a great Number of People [that] shall be utterly undone, and a great Multitude of the King's natural Subjects thereby fall into Idleness, to the great Impoverishment of the Realm'. With its customary sense of balance and fair play the British responded with an Act of Parliament (25 Henry VIII, 1533) preventing people from buying or owning 'wares made of Tin out of the Realm'. Wardens employed by the Worshipful Company were empowered to search for and confiscate such wares. Hawkers were prevented from selling them. Pewterers were forbidden to take on an 'Alien Apprentice'. No Pewterer 'shall be an Alien'. No Pewterer was allowed to go abroad 'to use teach or exercise the said craft of Pewterers upon pain to lose the Privilege and Benefit of an Englishman' and any currently abroad were given three months to return, or else suffer the same penalty. The Worshipful Company alone establishes standards, controls training of craftsmen and sets prices. To enforce such legislation nationwide must be a challenge but the message is clear: you don't mess with Pewterers. Such draconian policies enable the resumption of business as usual for a few hundred years.

industrial revolution introduced new practices and the use of alternative materials, the trade steadily declined. By the late Eighteenth Century the number of those in the Company who actually followed the trade was small.

Was tea really to blame for pewter's decline? It is hard to imagine drinking tea from pewter cups. How fully infused was Britain in the Eighteenth Century? Tea was available at this time as a luxury item imported from China for the well-to-do, its high price mainly the result of taxes, but it was much later when tea seeped into British lives; after the tea tax was commuted to a window tax in 1784 (which killed the profitable tea-smuggling trade); and also because of an act of industrial espionage undertaken by Robert Fortune, then head of Chelsea Physic Garden, who handed spade and clippers to Thomas Moore and, disguised as a Chinese peasant (complete with pigtail), smuggled tea-plants and expertise from China to India. Fifty years after his return, most tea came from India, the price had dropped and the quantity glugged per person had trebled.

Other authorities have suggested pewter reached its highest levels of production in the mid-Nineteenth Century. How to account for this discrepancy? The Worshipful Company was reluctant to accept innovative manufacturing methods of the kind that came to define the industrial revolution[1]. And experiments with the ingredients of pewter towards the end of the Eighteenth Century resulted in the development of a modified form of 'white metal' produced in sheets that were easy to work – without casting – into highly decorative designs. Traditionally, pewter objects had been cast in moulds, soldered, lathe-finished and polished. The Worshipful Company refused to accept the fancy new form of pewter, known

---

1 For example, John Duncumb's decision to introduce division of labour at his pewter works at Wribbenstall near Bewdley, which changed pewter-making there from craft to mass-production.

as Britannia metal. Nevertheless there was a strong demand for it, met unilaterally by factories in Birmingham and Sheffield. Here, at last, is the connection.

The *Atheneum* correspondent, William Costen Aitken, was quick to credit locals for innovations that led directly to his own independent discovery of the nature-printing process. Aitken, who spent much of his working life in manufacturing in the West Midlands, has a high regard for the technical skill and mechanical aptitude of this region and thinks it might be an inherited characteristic. He cites Richard Ford Sturges' method of decorating sheet metal, devised in 1851, in which lace or wire is placed between two sheets then run through a press; the results are made into ornamented tubes. A patent is taken out in January 1852, with 'the details open to investigation'. The notion inspires Aitken to experiment with Britannia metal. He concedes that 'it remains to be proved where the Austrians got their idea' but has sufficient brass neck to declare that 'the first natural objects were printed from in Birmingham' and 'nature-printing owes its recent successful progress to Birmingham'. George Wallis, another local, is willing to concede that a Danish goldsmith called Peter Kyhl had the basic conception long before anyone else but argues those in Vienna were 'much more likely to know of the existence of Kyhl's manuscript in the Royal Library at Copenhagen than a busy manufacturer at Birmingham'. Wallis is happy to defend Aitken's claim 'for the honour of Birmingham' on the basis the Austrians visited Birmingham after the Great Exhibition and that Sturges 'was not a man to hide his light under a bushel'. There is no evidence their paths crossed during the Austrians' visit to the 'Workshop of the World' but Wallis, like Aitken, is a man of 'strong conviction'. Where else could the Austrians have got the idea? As a line of argument, this is not entirely convincing. Why dismiss Vienna's frank admission of English influence in the form of those lace samples printed in Nottingham? And why award

Birmingham a monopoly on invention? If the thought could occur independently in Birmingham and in Copenhagen, why not also at Vienna? Aitken's claims to priority are less interesting to Pia than his working methods, of which he explains:

> Mr Bradbury and the Austrians arrived at their conclusion by a roundabout process of taking an impression on lead, and from the lead a copy by electro deposition, and a second plate by deposition, which formed that printed from; but the writer [Aitken] used Britannia metal, which is harder than lead, and printed from it direct, thereby securing details which are lost in taking two electro deposition plates.

This is enough for her to make plans to visit Birmingham with a view to finding out how good Aitken's work is – and to locate a source of Britannia metal.

Aitken would be shocked to learn that more than two-thirds of manufacturing jobs in the 'City of a Thousand Trades' have been lost since the late Seventies (equivalent in scale to those lost by Wales and Scotland combined during the same period) with all the problems that implies. Comparisons with Dagenham are unavoidable. The city centre feels emblematic of this sense of damage and loss, but things may be changing.

The library, a work of brutalist architecture by John Madin which some think a work of genius, is earmarked for demolition[1]. Pia reserved Aitken's works but only photocopies of the nature-prints are provided and there is some doubt as to whether the originals can be located. Beside the photocopies is a reprint of the obituary that appeared in the Birmingham Daily Post. It contains high praise, particularly where Aitken is credited with 'the invention of the beautiful process of Nature-printing'. There is also faint praise: 'Dumfries was too limited a field for Mr Aitken's peculiar powers'. And even veiled criticism: 'his brusqueness and sometimes eccentricity of speech and manner caused him now and then to be misunderstood by those who knew him little'. There is an account of a meeting of the Society of Arts at which Aitken delivered a lecture and made several caustic remarks about Bradbury who, he knew, was in the audience. Afterwards, Aitken remarked with satisfaction that 'Bradbury remained silent'.

It takes so long to sort out the photocopy problem that she has time to study ambitious plans for Birmingham: proposals for festivals, parks, museums, theatres, markets, places to 'hang out' and, above all, 'grit and authenticity'. Other cities in Britain (Liverpool, Manchester,

---

1 The replacement library, opened officially in 2013, took the public vote for Britain's favourite new building. A bronze statue by Gillian Wearing called *A Real Birmingham Family*, of local sisters Roma and Emma Jones holding hands with their young sons Kyan and Shaye, stands in front. The statue was cast in China.

Cardiff, Sheffield) have connected with their past through a similar pattern of urban regeneration. For Birmingham she wonders if this means building an 'olde quarter' from scratch, as has happened elsewhere; it will have to be a special kind of authenticity.

Among Aitken's papers are details of another of his singular projects. He was interested in demonstrating the unreliability of portrait paintings by comparing them with death-masks. As if portraiture was only ever concerned with accuracy of representation. The death-mask of Sir Walter Scott is produced as evidence, set against William Allan's painted portrait of the same man. And here, of all things, is a piece of cardboard cut to the size of Sir Walter Scott's hat to prove the artist wrong. It is further evidence of an aspiration of the age – to locate the objective image, as if verity requires a mechanical process. The use of death-masks with this precise aim was well underway in physiognomical studies and also in forensics to create records of the faces of unidentified bodies. Think of *L'Inconnue de la Seine*, the death-mask of a woman of astonishing beauty dragged from the river at Quai du Louvre in Paris in the 1880s. Many copies of the mask were made and it became a morbidly popular fixture in Parisian parlours. Albert Camus compared the mask's composed, enigmatic expression with that of the *Mona Lisa*. The enthusiasm for plastercasts, part of the democratisation of beauty, made real the ambition of art for all. Or think of the spectacular Cast Courts in the V&A, accessible versions of monumental works.

Sisi (the wife of Austrian Emperor, Franz Joseph) refused to sit for portraits after her thirty-second birthday and would not permit any photographs to be taken because she wanted to preserve the myth of her own beauty. She was assassinated at the age of sixty by an opportunist Italian anarchist. Her death mask in a glass cabinet at Bad Ischl presents a face unmarked by time, rather than a true likeness. So while it may be fair to compare the aesthetic qualities of a portrait painting and a face-mask, it feels unreasonable to disparage one for its lack of objectivity. Anyway, Aitken was a little late to the party. After seeing the daguerrotype in 1839 Paul de la Roche had declared 'painting is dead' and, by the time of Aitken's one-man campaign, art and science were already tumbling down different tunnels in pursuit of their own versions of truth.

Eventually the originals surface and they are worth the wait. One – of a fern – is titled DIRECT NATURE PRINTING. Under the heading in sepia copperplate is a formal explanation that says a good deal about Aitken's priorities:

> This plate was engraved and an impression printed from it in 2 minutes & 20 seconds, in the presence and on the occasion of HRH The Duke of Cambridge's visit to the Cambridge Street Works, Birmingham, June 2nd, 1857.

On some plates there is light tarnishing and other marks but overall it is high-quality work. Aitken claims it is possible to make at least five hundred prints from the same plate. Listen to the expert manufacturer. Trust him to develop a quick and an efficient system. He *is* on to something and he knows it, yet he never takes it any further. What is this about?

Auer is driven by the idea of a major polygraphic institute at the intellectual heart of Europe. Bradbury is a printer and publisher with an eye for the main chance. Aitken, on the other hand, is a run-of-the-mill polymath devoted to the industrial, scientific and artistic culture of the working people of Birmingham, with no special interest in print, publishing or botany. For him, nature-printing is about the technique, the metal and, sweeter still, the chance to big-up Birmingham at the expense of London and Europe.

* * *

The Pewter Sheet Company in Tyseley, a district of Birmingham, is a one-storey red-brick building on a corner opposite a terrace of pebbledash, satellite dishes and an upside-down England flag across an upstairs window. Coils of razor wire decorate its roof. Pia meets Chris, a worried man, in his small office at the back of the factory. A customer-led dispute (he calls it 'The Disaster') looms over the alleged adulteration of a composition. Perhaps one of the vats was not cleaned properly. He can't imagine how this could have happened. Rain drums on the roof. It hardly seems the time to discuss her requirements but she pushes on, explaining how while musing over the finer points of *A Practical Guide for the Manufacture of Metallic Alloys* (1876 edition) she had come to the conclusion that the make-up of alloys of Britannia metal is exceedingly variable, with each suitable for a specific purpose.

'This is the thing,' says Chris, glumly. 'Add a very small proportion of a given metal and you'll end up with another that has new and unexpected properties.'

How difficult it is to know exactly which formula was used by Aitken. Look at the *Practical Guide* and the problem is clear. Under the heading of Britannia metal are details of Algiers metal which consists of 90 parts tin and 10 parts antimony, but sometimes is made of 75 parts tin and 25 parts antimony. Then there is Argentin, which is 85.5 tin and 14.5 antimony. Ashberry metal contains tin, antimony and copper. The mix for Minofor includes tin, antimony, copper – and zinc. A small amount of bismuth is added to certain mixes, such as Plate Pewter. English metal is the most complex, with brass (made up of 75 copper and 25 zinc), plus nickel, bismuth, antimony and tungsten. All of these alloys come under the general heading of Britannia metal. And there are similar metals like English Tutania, which contains all of the same ingredients as Britannia metal in slightly different proportions. It's hard for a non-chemist to make sense of this stuff. Chris nods and shakes his head. 'The funny thing,' he says, without looking in the least amused, 'is that none of the mixes you mention comes close to the modern standard for Britannia metal, which is 92 tin, 6 antimony and 2 copper. The copper improves ductility and antimony makes it more malleable.' He glances at Pia and adds, 'They make it easier to stretch and squash.' And then suddenly Chris brightens. 'Did you know that the Oscars are still made of Britannia metal?' Even these days? How odd, since it has proved hard to find any other suppliers of Britannia metal. Like pewter, it isn't as popular as it used to be. 'Dunno what sort, though,' he adds, morosely.

The layout of the factory is similar to LeadAtom in Gosport – ladles, vats with pipes, ingots on workbenches. And Chris, too, gives her a souvenir of her visit in the form of sample sheets of his standard recipes, including one called Organ Mix made specifically for pipe-restoration of church organs. As a consequence of The Disaster he is unable to commit to any experimentation but tells her to keep in touch.

Pia changes at Moor Street to return to the shopping centre for the London connection. For part of the journey the train runs beside the Grand Union Canal, almost at the end of its journey from the docks at Limehouse. Ducks on the water, two determined ramblers on the towpath, and a blue narrow-boat. She has visited both ends now but is no nearer to a conclusion and decides Aitken's method is worth pursuing. If, that is, the sample plates are any use. If not, she will have to draw a line under pewter.

Nan

Pia is on a tea-break when Nan, a research volunteer in the Department of Typography and Graphic Communication, joins her. They are on friendly terms and Nan is one of the few who knows what Pia is up to. She asks about 'Bleak House'. Off-peak day-trips to Reading provide only a brief amount of studio time and have the awkward feel of a mercenary raid on resources. Staying over gives breathing space, so Pia resorts to spending some nights on campus in a subsidised hostel for visiting lecturers called Black Horse House. A shoebox-sized room, a bed on wheels, a foam-padded chair, a window in the ceiling and the slightly depressing, moulded plastic atmosphere of the 1970s. Never mind. It beats commuting – then again everything beats commuting. She tells Nan that 'Bleak House' is fine; how it is funny because while it has everything you need, nothing works properly.

Nan is watching her closely. 'And how is everything else?'

'Fine, fine.' Nan's eyes narrow. She is expecting more and Pia is not quite sure how to proceed. 'I guess I have to say' (or rather she does not; but today for some reason she does) 'that just being here is still a little difficult, at times.'

'Oh, dear. How's that?'

'I don't know. Everyone is very friendly. I suppose it's because I'm not on a course and don't have a proper role. I don't think I get in anyone's way and the space where I want to work is usually available but I feel like, if not an intruder then at least, an outsider.'

'I can see why you'd feel that way. I do, too, sometimes.'

Really? It's hard to believe. Everyone knows Nan. She has been working here for years. 'We're all so busy,' she says. 'No-one has time. How is your work going?'

Pia has to laugh. Nan has found the raw nerve. 'Things are terrible,' she says. 'How did you guess?'

'You don't usually stop for tea.'

This is true, although she has not really stopped for tea. She has just stopped. She tells Nan about Birmingham and how, for the last two days, she has tried to print the leaf of a plane tree using the pewter plates. Each of the plates takes an impression with a good level of detail, but it is not possible to print from them. The surface is too shiny and slippery and the plates slide under the rollers and the result is a smear and it's not fair. The prints all look like pictures of a falling leaf taken at a very slow shutter speed.

'That's an odd coincidence,' says Nan, as if it is just a conversation. 'I have been looking at printed paper leaves. During the War they were a common form of aerial propaganda.'

This change of direction throws Pia, but is welcome.

'Why leaves?'

'Oh I think they remind us all life is short, we'll soon be gone. For anyone but especially for a soldier, the falling leaf carries a poignant message.'

Perhaps this is part of what Pia likes so much about the fine tracery of nature-printed leaves. She hasn't really thought about it. Nan knows all about transient things. She works here in the Centre for Ephemera Studies, where she preserves and catalogues printed items never intended for posterity – labels, packets, tickets, timetables, stickers, certificates and so on. Gather these fragments and together they form a picture of their time. Pia tells Nan that her 'falling leaf' prints convey similar news: there is no future in pewter.

'But you have seen nature-prints made this way, so...'

Yes, it is possible, in theory. If the exact composition of the Britannia metal that WC Aitken used could be found, it would be simple. But she knows now that most manufacturers had their own recipes for Britannia metal. A contemporary analysis reveals many different formulas. Each version of Britannia metal has its own properties and at least one is good for nature-printing. Unfortunately, it is not one she has been given. In *The Practical Guide to Metallic Alloys* is an old German proverb that she recites for Nan:

Speech is silvern, silence is golden.
To say one thing and mean another is Britannia metal.

Britannia metal is a mixed-up thing and there is no chance of finding out what Aitken used for his plates. Pewter is decidedly not the way to avoid Victorian science.

'In that case,' says Nan, 'do something else. How about supper with an old woman?'

* * *

Later that evening Nan explains ephemera – which consists of virtually all printed matter with the exception of books, music and maps.

'There have always been specialist collectors of cigarette cards and beermats and whatnot, but we are the first to attempt the subject in its entirety.'

To gather, organise and ultimately to make sense of so much intrinsically worthless stuff will be a library of Babel, a vast and complex undertaking for generations of scholars. And yet it is extraordinary to think that to date it has not been properly accounted for, or catalogued.

'We're like collectors, compelled to impose our small sense of order on chaos.'

Nan is working on wine labels, cataloguing the extensive collection of a lecturer at the university, recently deceased; his habit was to remove the labels from bottles after consuming their contents. At the rate of two or three per night he managed to acquire thousands before his liver succumbed.

'Such diligence,' sighs Nan, with a slight lift of her glass. 'It will take me years to sort them all out: vintage, country of origin, vineyard, grape, colour.'

The lecturer's wine labels chart the progress of a life, forming a nostalgic assortment that probably, like a shoebox of family snaps, was seldom revisited. They were stored as evidence, objects that defined a sense of identity. Collecting is a record of our interests, who we are, or who we want to be; and this is why it seems sometimes like a quest for perfection. There are collectors of Lottery scratchcards who never scratch the cards as part of their compulsion to preserve a pristine, undamaged world. Collecting often suggests a need for completeness and for order that is never satisfied, that drives knowledge. It is no coincidence that those who know most about nature-printing are, to a greater or a lesser extent, collectors of nature-prints. An inevitable side-effect of dedicated collecting is expertise. The conversation drifts hazily in the direction of nature-printing. Nan knows a little about the problems with lead. If pewter is unworkable, what's next? Pia begins to bluster, explaining how Auer made copper plates from lead originals through a procedure called electrotyping. And how Bradbury said that 'the art of Nature-Printing could not have been developed without the printing power of the electrotype'.

'I'm not sure how it's done, but I have a feeling it will be way beyond my capabilities and resources.'

Nan isn't so easily intimidated. 'I don't see why. But why do it yourself, anyway? After all, electroplating is still quite common.'

It may be late and Pia's mind may be a little slurry but this strikes her as a revelation on several counts. It is as if a psychological block has been removed. In the first place (amazingly) she had not made a connection between electrotyping and electroplating and in any case she had not considered the possibility that the method was still current. The idea that she might sub-contract this part of the job had never crossed her mind either.

There is one notable figure in the story of nature-printing to whom all others concede precedence. A goldsmith from Denmark called Peter Kyhl is unquestionably the first to have made nature-prints according to the principles later developed and popularised by the Viennese State Printing-office. The part of Sweden where Pia grew up is closer to Copenhagen than Stockholm, geographically and in spirit, so she is familiar with the place. There is a tenuous affinity with Peter Kyhl. They have each encountered some of the same difficulties. He talked about the problems of working with lead, explaining that 'the utmost care must be used, as every trifle, however small, such as hairs and dust, [is] printed together with the object itself'. Though the difference between discovery and rediscovery is significant, both know what it is like to stumble along in a Scandinavian darkness.

The Kyhl affair broke just as Vienna's publicity machine had gathered enough momentum to penetrate the far reaches of Europe, as shown by the announcement of the new nature-printing process in the May 20, 1853 edition of *Berlingske Tidende*[1]. Eleven days later Professor Thiele promoted Peter Kyhl's claims in the same journal, explaining that Kyhl had devised this method of printing twenty years earlier, in 1833, but died before being able to develop it further. At this point Dr Mehren, the author of the original article on Auer's innovation, decided to intervene. He wrote to Vienna endorsing Auer, enclosing both articles and Kyhl's notes.

Auer is quick to publish all of the information together with a careful riposte. A clear case of damage limitation. Unwilling to lose the honour of the discovery, Auer rearranges the sequence of the articles and begins by accepting Dr Mehren's comforting view that

---

1 This Danish newspaper, founded in 1749, predates *The Times* by some forty years and is one of the oldest in the world.

although Kyhl came first 'the honour of this invention [is Auer's and]... cannot be diminished in any way by this circumstance, as [Kyhl's has] always remained hidden and unpractised'. Auer provides the text of Thiele's letter and Kyhl's notes, then offers an illuminating commentary. Kyhl's work amounts to 'an interesting essay, a fine experiment' but Auer emphasises that it is not on the same level as 'our invention' which 'differs from that of Kyhl as much as day from night'. Auer is stretching a point as he had not seen Kyhl's work, but the distinction between having a good idea and bringing it to full expression is valid and it comes up repeatedly in different contexts during the period. What is strange is the way ideas seem to coalesce in the atmosphere at certain moments in time. Abstract entities take shape, are seen and are wrestled to earth by different people in different places. For example, Alfred Russel Wallace made a similar point when comparing his letter on the theory of natural selection with Darwin's work on the same subject. Wallace was happy to concede the honour of the discovery to Darwin. Likewise Joseph Wilson Swan and Walter Woodbury never could agree on who discovered the fundamentals of the Woodburytype process, but Woodbury was the first to *apply* the principles.

Auer claimed that his own system was able to convert anything to printing-forms, whereas Kyhl 'knew only how to stamp flat objects into harder metal'. It is a curious coincidence that all of those who attempted nature-printing chose to print more-or-less the same things and most had a relatively two-dimensional surface. Pia's friends have teased her over her 'obsession with flat things.' The subjects of Kyhl's prints ('leaves, linen and woven stuffs... laces, feathers of birds, scales of fishes and serpentskins') are remarkably similar to those of Auer, with one or two exceptions (agates, fossils; that bat). Kyhl's method predated commercial application of the invention of electrotyping and the introduction of gutta-percha and so from Auer's perspective must have seemed primitive. He believed that Kyhl used either a hard metal incapable of receiving a detailed impression or a soft metal suitable only for a limited number of copies that would prove of little benefit to 'the public at large or the numberless participators of science'. And if Kyhl's process was so good, why had it been disregarded for so long? Wasn't it the case that Kyhl's work, languishing in Copenhagen, could 'be looked on as nearly not existing'? This seems a little hard on Denmark. Even so, when Thiele countered that all of Kyhl's work is 'exposed to public inspection in the collection of engravings in this town', it is difficult to suppress a smile.

It would be relatively easy for Pia to explore the archives in Copenhagen and she plans to visit on her way to Sweden at Christmas. Then the weather deteriorates, snow lies deep and crisp and even on the runways at Heathrow and no-one is going anywhere, which creates predictable havoc. On the day of her departure it is apparent that she will miss her scheduled appointment with the Kunstbibliothek. Rather than mope at the airport she decides, armed with her hard luck travel story and a bottle of wine, to visit a companion who has no plans for Christmas.

The friend lives in an eight-storey commercial block just off Broadway Market in E9, close by Regent's Canal. At ground level there are still a few light-industrial units, lock-ups and garages. Most have disappeared as galleries and art collectives invade the latest edgy urban space. Pia has never paid them much attention but today notices a sign – *Perfect Plating, Since* 1973 – on the far side of the car-park and decides to take a closer look. It is hard to see anything by peering through the grimy window but she must be visible from the other side because someone steps out and asks if they can help. The owner, Trevor, ushers her in to the front office. A desk, two white plastic garden chairs, a yellowing computer, cardboard boxes of various sizes and a threadbare sofa against the wall weighed down with a heap of door handles. He waves his arms.

'Apologies for the mess. It's been hectic, lately.' His words echo in the room. They sit in the plastic chairs on either side of the desk. 'We don't usually get involved with handles,' he says, nodding at them. 'Usually it's silver plate and jewellery.'

'Oh, so you don't do electro-plating with copper,' says Pia, with unexamined relief.

'We do,' he says. 'Or, well, let me make a call. It's pretty straight-forward. Let me call Tel.' And he does call Tel. It's a peculiar situation. They face one another as Trevor discusses her case. At a certain point the conversation drifts to other matters. Trevor stands and paces the room. She is about to make her apologies and leave when he wraps things up.

'It *is* straightforward,' he affirms. 'Bring in a plate before Christmas and we'll have it coppered by the new year.'

And all for £50. What has she got to lose? For the answer to that question she traipses through a warren of artists' studios to her friend's 'office'. You are not allowed to live here and so of course no-one does, but if you do visit take care opening cupboards in case a mattress topples out with the stiff force of a stage show.

'Fifty pounds!' exclaims her friend. 'You're going to give fifty pounds to some geezer with a garage. It must be the season of goodwill.'

He's right, the festive mood has infected Pia. She believes the chance meeting might be the work of fate busily unloading compensation long overdue – not just for the flight delay but also for the inadequacies of lead and pewter. Early next morning she is back at *Perfect Plating* with her piece of lead. Terms are agreed, cash on delivery. Trevor wishes her a Merry Christmas and she heads for the airport. Overnight the freezing fog has lifted. The runways are clear and planes are shuffling out of Heathrow; one bound for Copenhagen with her on board.

Scandinavia is seldom inconvenienced by snow but today the weather is unusually severe. Many roads are blocked, cars are buried entirely and there are no trains across the bridge to Sweden. The taxi driver takes Pia to two hotels near the centre that (with biblical inevitability) are full before she gets third time lucky. Next day is Christmas Eve and she hurries to the Kunstbibliothek only to find that in common with most of Denmark it is closed until the New Year. By then, she will be back in the UK. Peter Kyhl will have to wait. On a positive note, her parents call to say the trains are running.

* * *

Even though it is closed to the public, life for everyone at the Garden is busy during the winter months. New garden areas are constructed, beds are relaid and planted, educational initiatives are planned, projects and exhibitions and courses finalised. The reverberations from these activities reach the design team in the shape of an urgent requirement for all kinds of brochures, books, signage, web pages and even for retail items such as preserve labels and tea-towels. There is little time to think about nature-printing in relation to her forthcoming course. And then she receives news that her copper-plated lead is ready for collection.

Nothing appears to have moved in the room since her last visit, including Trevor. There are the handles on the sofa.

'Sorry it's taken so long. It's been hectic since Christmas.' She nods and agrees that time has been short. 'Looks good, don't it?' says Trevor. On the table is a coppered plate that gleams dully. It does look good. A layer of copper, thin as varnish, covers the lead entirely. This should harden the plate, remove the oxidisation problem and allow Pia to make a large number of prints without loss of detail. Copper is a standard medium for printing plates that does not react with inks or with cleansing agents. She should be able to say goodbye to the grubby marks that have characterised all of her work to date.

The extent to which Bradbury was an inebriate (as alleged by Auer) is hard to judge, if only because his own works and writings show him to be remarkably clear-headed, especially in those early years spent building a reputation as a nature-printer; as when, having set the blue touch-paper alight, he took a step back. While Auer exploded, Bradbury concentrated on his first project: *A few leaves represented by 'Nature-Printing' showing the application of the art for the reproduction of botanical and other natural objects. With a delicacy of detail and truthfulness to nature unobtainable by any other known method of printing.* A promotional effort, then; a large unbound portfolio consisting eventually of thirty-nine different plates sold singly at 1/6d, or in sets of twenty-one for 21/-; mostly of wild flowers, plus five ferns and a sprig from a Lime tree. Excerpts from the press in praise of nature-printing comprise the only significant text page. One of the quotes, taken from *The Times*, refers to Auer's work. Bradbury was happy to take the credit.

Upon publication, reviews were mixed and polite questions asked about the adequacy of the process for certain kinds of work. In general, the leaves have printed well but the flowers are flattened and as a result their precise shape is hard to determine; furthermore, the stamens and styles dominate at the expense of the transparent petals. One or two of the examples used for printing were imperfect. It is impossible to discern the unusual structure of Common Milkwort's flowers in the red splodges that are printed. The flowers of Common Hare's-ear are very dark green splats. On Meadowsweet and Common Golden Rod the shape of the flowers cannot be discerned, although their position and arrangement is clear enough. Ferns are well-printed – but if nature-printing cannot reproduce fruits and flowers with absolute fidelity, what use is it to science and botany at a time when the main approach to classification of plants is based on morphology?

Bradbury printed no more flowers, but the comments inspired him to criticise Auer who, he said, 'claimed for Nature-Printing a position to which it has not right...[the process] still has its defects, it has its limits and its applications are limited, and care will be required to confine it within the bounds of its capabilities.'

William Hooker, Director of Kew Gardens, was unconvinced about nature-printing and as he explained a few years later in a letter to Talbot:

> What we want now of days, is not only a representation of the
> plant, but the analysis of the fructification, venation &c,
> in magnified figures. This is a great desideratum too in
> 'Nature-printing' – &, there besides, is the defect arising from
> inequality of surface in the plant; & where there is pubescence,
> & fructification – all that is blurred.

Other botanists did not share all of Hooker's doubts about nature-printing. Joseph Hooker, William's son, remarked that 'some of the plates seem to surpass the specimens themselves in elegance and in colouring'. Thomas Moore praised the mechanical reproduction of detail in the preface to *The Nature-Printed British Ferns*, but the nature-prints in this book were accompanied by engravings from detailed sketches of particular parts of ferns. Moore also observed that the variations found among plants:

> often serve to connect the individuals into a series so extended,
> and withal so complete, that the so-called species themselves seem
> to lose all definite limit... these so-called species of plants are but
> groups of individuals having a certain amount of resemblance...
> Nature seems to acknowledge only the individual, while the
> species... is an artificial thing of man's contrivance[1].

---

1 Moore's preface, written in August 1859, came barely a month after Alfred Wallace's groundbreaking essay On The Tendency of Varieties to Depart Indefinitely From The Original Type was presented at the Linnean Society.

William Hooker objected to nature-printing and mechanical objectivity for precisely this reason: the difficulty of recognising all the features of a type of plant from an individual example. Daston and Galison explain in *Objectivity*:

> As long as botanists insisted on figures that represented the characteristic form of a species or even genus, photographs and other mechanical images of individual plants in all their particularity would have little appeal.

The Viennese botanist Ettingshausen did not believe nature-prints were identical with the original plants but unlike William Hooker he valued the highly detailed rendering of surface texture. Moore agreed that 'its accuracy is perfect as far as it goes...the outline and the venation...if it fails, as it does, to give the details of the sori, and their indusia, it accurately gives the general form and arrangement even of these parts.'

Leaving aside concerns over the imperfect presentation of the flowers and the facts that the greens of a few stems are too dark and certain other colour choices are questionable, the plates still retain an unearthly beauty. On the back of *A few leaves* Bradbury was admitted to the Royal Institution. Membership invested his work with credibility and provided a platform from which he delivered a lecture on nature-printing and a stunning attack on Auer.

For his lecture Bradbury lifted passages on the history of nature-printing directly from Chevalier von Perger's poorly translated article in Auer's *Entdeckung des Naturselbstdruckes* (Discovery of the Natural Self-Printing Process). A typically audacious strategy. Where Perger suggests direct nature-prints are 'durable' but 'defective' because 'the production could only take place very slowly, as the blacking of the plants with the printer's balls robbed much time...', we find Bradbury also believes direct impressions are 'durable' yet 'defective' and that 'the production of impressions could only take place very slowly, as the blackening of the plants with the printer's ball required much time...'. Perger explained that dried plants were:

held over the smoke of an oil-lamp, or over a candle, till they were blackened all over in an equal manner, then they were placed between soft paper and rubbed over with the smoothing-bone until the soot was imparted to the paper.

Bradbury's handling of dried plants is equally careful:

By holding them over the smoke of a candle, or an oil lamp, they became blackened in an equal manner all over, and by being placed between two soft leaves of paper, and being rubbed down with a smoothing-bone, the soot was imparted to the paper.

Finally, Bradbury is prepared to go to some lengths to sort out tangled Viennese thinking. The language of Perger was clunky:

Thus we find already in the year 1572 in the *Book on Art* of Alexis Pedemontanus, brought into German by Wecker the first hints on the process of making impressions of plants; we read in the *Journal des voyages* by M. de Moncoys, that about the year 1660 the Dane Welkenstein gave instruction in the making of plants; Linné tells us (in his *Philosophia botanica*) that in America a certain Hessel (1707) made such impressions, and later (1728-1757) it was especially Professor Kniphof at Erfurt who occupied himself so much with that work that, in conjunction with the bookseller Funke, he established a proper printing-office for this purpose.

In comparison, Bradbury's historical account is sparklingly well-organised:

> In the *Book of Art* of Alexis Pedemontanus (printed in the year 1572) and translated into German by Wecker, may be found the *first* recorded hint as to taking impressions of plants. At a later period – in the *Journal des Voyages* by M. de Moncoys, in 1650 it is mentioned that one Welkenstein, a Dane, gave instruction in making impressions of plants. Linneas, in his *Philosophica Botanica*, relates that in America, in 1707, impressions of plants were made by Hessel; and later (1728-1757), Professor Kniphof, at Erfurt, (who refers to the experiments of Hessel) in conjunction with the bookseller Funke, established a printing-office for this purpose.

Having impressed his London audience with the depth of his knowledge Bradbury suggests Austria had long been aware of Kyhl's work. (Bradbury's knowledge of Kyhl, of course, came from Auer's account.) He said that the Staatsdruckerei almost certainly stole patented ideas from the English – men of the calibre of Sturges, Branson and Aitken. Furthermore, he argues that all the main features of the process, such as the electrotype, were in use already. Granted Worring (not Auer) might be credited with introducing soft lead, but 'it cannot in truth be allowed, that he who accidentally happens to possess the means to mature a system, even though he add some features, is the inventor'. Bradbury then storms the moral high ground, echoing *The Atheneum*'s point that 'personal allegations' and 'vituperative allusions' have no place in a civilised debate. And yet he is prepared to state, without compunction:

> It is evident, that, in more instances than one, Councillor Auer, who has arrogated to himself the <u>sole</u> discovery of

Nature-Printing, has given proof of a selfish and unfair desire to aggrandise himself at the expense of others: his passion for fame has led him even beyond the warrantable bounds of propriety.

It is Pretsch 'to whom [Auer] owes most of his present high position by reason of his energetical and practical and even scientifical capability'. Bradbury also cites the case of Anton Hartinger who, it is said, gave up his position at the Staatsdruckerei because his Prize medal for chromolithography at the Great Exhibition was retained by Auer on behalf of the Printing-office. This sounds plausible but it isn't necessarily so. Hartinger, the artist responsible for the artwork and colour plates in *Endlicher's Paradisus Vindonbonensis* (Vienna Paradise) might, without good reason, have felt hard done by. Certain plates were shown at the Exhibition but the giant work was not published until 1860, years after Bradbury's lecture; and the book's introduction has a different perspective. Hartinger's initial attempts at making prints of his gold medal-winning artworks tried 'the patience, the skill and the purse of the experimentalist' and yielded only 'disparaging remarks'. To help Hartinger Auer 'generously placed a press at his disposal' and all problems were soon resolved.

Bradbury is silent on the subject of his own behaviour and motivation at Vienna. He does not comment directly on Auer's book. Taken at face value, his own lecture is a masterpiece: informative, provocative and wholly convincing. As more of a coup de grâce than a compliment, the published edition of the speech was dedicated:

To ALOIS AUER – director of the imperial court and governor of the imperial printing office at Vienna, etc etc. In memory of his sojourn at Vienna, and studies in the establishment over which he presides, this monograph of the art of nature printing is dedicated by Henry Bradbury.

The coppered plate on the workbench gleams up at her, if a little more dully than before. Pia reminds herself that hardly anyone has tried to make prints in this way for more than one hundred and fifty years. The sense of an imminent breakthrough persists together with an equally strong feeling that something is about to go wrong and it is just a question of when.

On the plus side the answer to the question (when?) arrives without delay. Wiping excess ink from the plate, bright flecks appear on the scrim; microscopic constellations auguring disaster. A dab of white spirit makes a metallic smear and after a couple of minutes she has a clean lead plate and a rag impregnated with fifty pounds of copper.

'What you get from a geezer with a garage,' she mutters. Her voice quivers unexpectedly.

'It is only a minor catastrophe,' says Martin Andrews, who happens to be nearby. 'You are on the right track. There are companies that can supply proper copper rather than this...spray paint.'

Pia laughs bitterly and bins the scrim. The electrodeposition companies she has found are too large to be interested in working with individuals, or are reluctant to experiment, or just do not want to work with lead. Martin says he knows someone who might be interested at a firm of electroplaters that holds a Royal Warrant, but the news barely registers. Before this setback Pia thought she had shaken off her fear of electrotyping. After all, it is just plating.

'Just plating!' exclaims Martin. 'This is changing base metals into gold. It is alchemy on an industrial scale.' Galvanoplasty (yet another name for electroplating) is an early marvel of electricity, one which predated the lightbulb by several decades. A Birmingham company, H & GR Elkington, swept up patents and controlled the English electroplating market from the 1840s until the end of the Nineteenth Century. Among other things it created fine reproductions of antiquities. Prince Albert visited and was fascinated by the procedure. A red rose dipped in a vat changed to gold before his eyes. On the flower were tangled gold threads of cobweb.

'This galvanised Albert to set up an electroplating studio at Buckingham Palace.'

Picture the figure of Albert seated on his throne in Kensington Gardens covered in bright gold, still holding the Great Exhibition catalogue. Is this the man himself, a latterday Midas? The appeal of electroplating was not the gold – Albert had enough of that, already – but the idea of combining high art with mechanical skill to make attractive objects available to all for a moderate price. As factory owner George Elkington put it:

> Facsimiles of the antique and the various works of art which are at present confined to the collections of the amateur may be now produced in the noble metals [which is] the most efficient means of spreading fine taste, and of educating the public mind to a due appreciation of the really beautiful.

Well possibly, assuming the public mind cares for such things. The notion of art for everyone in the age of mechanical reproduction raises other questions. Where, for example, does this leave the work of art? If there is no discernible difference between innumerable copies of a Grecian urn and the original, the significance of the latter must be diluted; though according to German philosopher Walter Benjamin the original has an 'aura', a unique existence in time and space. A fine distinction. 'Think of it this way,' says Martin, and he quotes Keats:

> Thou still unravish'd bride of quietness
> Thou foster-child of Silence and slow Time.

'These lines can't apply to the reproduction on your mantelpiece. Only the original, still in its own space, has this intangible presence.'

Pia does not have a Grecian urn or even a mantelpiece but knows it is true – the stuff that we buy in museum gift shops often seems out of place in the context of our lives. The emergence of technologies that make Grecian urns available to all results in unexpected tensions. This is the moment when Science and Industry come together with machinery able to create the exact, reasonably priced reproduction. A brilliant breakthrough and yet, as far as its own works are concerned, Art replies that it isn't enough; that it misses the point. Nature-prints strive to side with technology, but the method of production is laborious and from the outset they are far from cheap. The price of Bradbury's book of ferns is equivalent to more than £300 in today's money. Very few people are willing to spend so much on a book, even if the prints, according to *The Times*, 'appear as if the original specimens were pasted on the paper.' Nature-printing may have been developed as a method of mechanical reproduction but the quality of work carries it to a different place altogether; and might explain why, at its best, it retains a particular beauty. Printing from a leaf gives an impression of its shape and structure. Whether or not it is any good depends on the skill of the printer. Likewise the quality of a photograph depends not only on the skill of the photographer but also on decisions made in the darkroom. In both cases the result is a likeness, an artful fiction, and the ideal of the objective image an exercise in wishful thinking.

* * *

To her surprise, Martin does make an appointment for Pia to visit an electroplating company near Kew on the urban edge of Metroland. She has become a connoisseur of industrial estates and can tell this is an early example. The buildings are grand and sprawling and proclaim the importance of the companies that put them there. Most impressive is the Art Deco Hoover building (now a Tesco). The firm she seeks occupies a typically superior red-brick unit and here she meets James, a technical expert now semi-retired and at one remove from the usual commercial pressures. He has a personal interest in the nature-printing project, though the company considers it too small to be considered an opportunity.

'As far as I can tell,' says James, studying the plate, 'you are more interested in electroforming – or electrotyping, as it was once known. If you just want to cover lead with copper, it can be done. And in such a way that the copper stays on the lead. That's electroplating.' He smiles to reveal Martin has not held back details of her recent experience. 'But if you want a separate copper replica of the lead plate, that is electroforming.' At last the exact meanings of these words is clear. And it turns out electroplating is still an important process for precious metals. Silver is used not only for tableware but also for electrical contacts, while bathroom fittings and gas holders are plated with gold. Electroforming is big business, too, and copper is employed extensively, particularly in the manufacture of electronic components, industrial products and parts for musical instruments. 'Eighty-five thousand tons of copper were used world-wide last year in this manner, equivalent to sixteen miles of fully loaded articulated lorries.'

'So it is possible,' says Pia to herself, 'to make a copper plate from my lead.'

'Almost anything can be electroformed from a master, so yes, it is possible. Even the moulds for chocolate bars are often copper electroforms from a steel mandrel, or mould. But it would be useful to have some more details.' James would like to know the required thickness of the plate and he would also like to know exactly what the plate should look like. He isn't the only one. Pia is visiting Vienna shortly and will return with pictures. In the meantime he promises to undertake experiments with her 'bit of roofing lead'.

* * *

A few days later Pia takes delivery of a small package: James's first attempt at an intaglio copper plate from the lead she had provided, bearing an image of three oak leaves. One of the leaves is faint, the edges barely visible. She calls James to talk things over. He is reluctant to go into detail, says only that her 2mm lead was glued to a slightly larger wood block and the surface prepared 'in the usual way'.

The result is a plate that resembles, in cross-section, a barbershop boater hat. The brim is formed from the wood, the side-band is the depth of the lead plate and the crown tip is the printing surface. This presents a small problem. The plate will squash if it is run through a press. 'Yes,' says James, 'I did wonder about that. It's difficult when you don't have a model to refer to.'

There has to be another way to learn about this electro-business and Pia has discovered an expert who runs courses on the subject in Leeds. His workshop is not far from the station, tucked away down a narrow alley behind the restored Corn Exchange. She presses a buzzer and the door is half-opened almost immediately by a tall thin man in his early forties who cups a cigarette loosely in his free hand. The smoke coils around the sleeve of his jacket. He blinks at her and it appears neither of them knows quite what to expect.

'Pia?' he asks, glancing nervously over her shoulder as if to make sure there are no others.

'Simon Jones?' she replies, completing the strangeness of the introduction.

They shake hands and she edges into a cramped hallway of boxes, coats, shoes and other less easily identifiable stuff. There is time for a quick tour. Upstairs his girlfriend makes costumes. In the centre of her space is a mountain of fabrics. Simon's room – part workshop, part laboratory, part storeroom – is just as chaotic. Two large workbenches are strewn with tools, brushes, beakers, boxes, tins, coils of cable, bobbins of copper and silver wire, reels of tape, bottles and bags of chemicals. In one corner is a two-ring electric hob with two filthy pans used for anything but food. He shows her tools for polishing, for soldering and welding. Here is a bench grinder and here a lathe, a drill-press, a fly-press, a full lost wax vacuum set-up, and here is equipment for casting and electroplating. She notes acid baths, anodising tanks, vats of different coloured liquids. On shelves over a line of tanks are various enamel-grey rectifiers for controlling current and temperature. Other shelves are packed with boxes, files, bottles, books. There are meters, counters, dials, digital thermometers, switches labelled 'heat' and 'agitate'. If all of this is in regular use – and apparently, it is – then Simon must be a virtuoso.

'Welcome to the sweatshop,' he says, with a slightly sour laugh.

This will be no ordinary course. There is no schedule. As suspected, she is the sole registrant. By way of introduction he shows various items, evidence of his considerable prowess in the manufacture of military accoutrements – buttons, badges, medals, coins, jewellery, plus epaulettes, tassels and plumes; and examples of frankly bizarre headdress. All are perfect copies. Simon used to work in a shady niche of the antiques trade, specialising in forgeries. This bothered him so he left, preferring the honest fakery of costume jewellery. Finally, he started his own company. He supplies museums, collectors, societies involved in re-enactments, film companies, Savile Row tailors, even the Royal household. While he talks, the phone rings. It continues to ring repeatedly through the day and he continues to ignore it.

'You must be very busy.'

He nods and with a scowl mutters cryptically, 'I'm a maker, not a businessman,' then he pulls up two chairs at a workbench. 'What do you know?'

Those who studied chemistry at school would be familiar with the concept of electrolysis. The object to be plated has a negative charge. The plating material and the ions in solution have a positive charge. Switch the current on and the positive ions are attracted to the negative electrode. Pia has researched early methods of electrotyping (or electroforming!) in abstruse technical journals at Reading and has followed the history of the process from the moment in 1800 when Volta wrote to Joseph Banks with news of his pile. She knows that a casual remark by Warren de la Rue (son of the founder of the firm of security printers) set the ball rolling in September, 1836. He had been working with a new battery devised by John Frederic Daniell (the Daniell cell) that delivered a regular supply of current and observed that:

the copper plate is also covered with a coating of metallic copper which is continually being deposited; and so perfect is the sheet of copper thus formed that, being stripped off, it has the polish and even a counterpart of every scratch of the plate on which it is deposited.

A regular supply of current is key to obtaining a uniform deposition of metal. This revelation inspires Moritz von Jacobi, a Russian professor teaching in Estonia, to the discovery of an effective method of electroplating, although (naturally) others dispute his claim to priority. By 1840, Jacobi's monograph on the subject, *Die Galvanoplastik*, has been translated to English. This and other developments lead directly to Elkington's mastery of electroplating. It occurs to her that Elkington, like Simon, made military badges and buttons.

'But Elkington was a businessman,' says Simon, ruefully. 'Anyway, history and theory are fine as far as they go. You can't beat a practical demonstration.' As he says this his eyes light up, because it suddenly occurs to him that he can take on one of many outstanding jobs. 'Get some real work done for a change.' What follows is a breathtaking technical performance in which her role is that of spectator. When she attempts to take notes Simon shakes his head, tells her it is unnecessary. He is preparing detailed fact-sheets to send in due course. (In point of fact she never hears from him again. Fortunately, she continues to jot things down.) Work proceeds at such a pace it is hard to keep track. Thirteen mould-made buttons are strung on copper wire and attached to a small plating rack – a rectangle of titanium 'straws' with small hooks welded to the transverse sides to hold the wire. The two verticals extend at the top and welded to them are flat copper hangers. Most of the surface is coated with insulating polypropylene to prevent the accretion of metal on the rack. 'First job: degrease the metal. Has to be absolutely clean. Caustic soda works. I prefer something a little stronger.' They move over to the cooker. He tips powder in a pan and a solution is soon bubbling on the stove. Pia checks the label of his sodium metasilicate degreasing agent and sees that in case of any contact including inhalation the advice is to seek medical attention immediately. Simon is leaning over the pan dunking the frame of buttons like a teabag. 'Smoking inadvisable,' he says with a smoker's humour, cigarette hanging from his lip. 'Should have proper ventilation in here, too.' The buttons are rinsed in a tub of cold water at his feet, scrubbed with a toothbrush, then dipped in a large white bucket of greenish solution of nickel chloride. Nickel will help to hold the gold and also prevent it from tarnishing. Apparently it is important to know what metals stick properly to other metals, the perfect cue for Pia's 'geezer in a garage' story. Simon isn't surprised. 'Hardly anyone knows how to make anything, these days,' he mutters. Across the top of the bucket are three titanium rods wired to a power unit. The central rod is the negatively charged cathode from which Simon hangs the rack of buttons. Tabs of nickel are suspended from the positively charged anodes on either side. When the current is switched on the solution begins to fizz. He starts at a low voltage and increases it gradually. Thickness and weight of deposit are controlled by such things as: temperature, time, strength of current, quality of solution, proximity of the electrodes to one another, the surface area of the item to be plated, additional trace elements in the solution, and so on. Any miscalculation leads to an uneven deposition across the surface, or rippling, or cracking. From a commercial perspective it is important to know how much of every precious metal is used for plating in order to know how much to charge. He uses a complex spreadsheet program to monitor all of these variables and promises to send Pia a copy... The nickel-plated buttons are rinsed and then a similar operation is repeated with a bucket of blue solution labelled 9k GOLD. As he is working he explains that his aim is to replicate items as closely as possible by deploying the techniques of those expert craftsmen of yore.

'The stuff you see at craft fairs is mostly junk. Home-made, not hand-made. Beads on a string. You don't expect a jeweller to have a mine in the basement but should expect more than the ability to polish stones and stick bits together like Lego.'
He expands on this theme, turning to his own problems.

'As Thomas Carlyle said, "there is nothing that some man cannot make a little worse and sell a little cheaper and he who considers only the price is that man's lawful prey". Factories and machines do the basics efficiently but they're not interested in making things well – they just want to make things cheaply. It's impossible to compete on cost, so I must make things better. The market for high-quality work, alas, is very small.'

The parallels with Pia's own project have not escaped her. It isn't just that nature-printing never is as efficient as its advocates claim. In the end, excessive expenditure costs Auer his job, and might have cost Bradbury his life. Simon is right: to be competitive in the main-stream requires a cost-effective approach to mass-production and is not a question of beauty, accuracy, or quality. If early ambitions for nature-printing focused on mass-production, it proved a fatal error. How will the demand for unique fine prints of ferns and plants compare with the market for military regalia? A connection she never expected to make.

Simon switches off and lifts the sparkling gold buttons out of the solution. Rinsing for the final time, his lamentations rise to a crescendo. 'We don't make things any more. No ships in the shipyard, no mines anywhere. No steel, no cars, industrial estates devoid of industry.' (Pia knows this isn't true, but decides not to quibble.) 'The country's broke, but if you need anything there's the pound shop. What do you think?'

Pia thinks he is asking about the buttons. They look very good, although there is little chance of remembering how they were made. Her impression is that while the theory is comprehensible, mastery depends on a deep understanding of chemicals, metals and electricity. Without such knowledge it would be more than brave to take on electroplating. A better approach might be to collaborate with Simon, or to persuade him to visit Reading to set up a studio there. When she floats this idea he appears to give it thought and suggests without any sense of irony, wholly oblivious to the plaintive cries of the workshop phone, that she give him a call. In the weeks that follow she does call, many times...

The ringing, the fumes and the intensity of the morning have left a dull ache at the centre of her forehead. So far the course has only scratched the gold-plated surface of the man's expertise. Even so, Pia needs a break. A strong coffee and a brisk stroll through the Corn Exchange and the Victorian arcades restores her senses. The city centre is busy with shoppers and already the bars are crowded with the vanguard of Saturday night, knots of hair-straightened girls in micro-skirts and packs of close-cropped boys in tight-fitting shirts and creased trousers. Back at the workshop Simon studies a lead plate. They discuss the idea of electroforming and Pia asks a question she had prepared in advance. A copper plate made from the lead must be in relief, with the veins of the leaf standing proud. To print intaglio, as she must, it will be necessary to make a second plate from the first, so the same veins are recessed. How can a new copper plate be made directly on an existing copper plate? Surely once formed they would be inseparable?

'There are always ways. Remember that.' He waves wearily at the bowing shelves of books and box-files. 'Maybe coating the first plate with a film of silver iodide, or similar; that would probably work as a releasing agent.'

One afternoon is not long enough to make both copper plates but Simon is willing to prove his nonconformist approach by showing a different path to the intaglio stage via a silicone mould, an enticing offer that puts his audience on the edge of its seat. Silicone seems like a modern form of gutta-percha. The effortless brilliance with which he settles to the work makes Pia feel envious. He rummages through drawers, finds half of a shallow plastic cigar box stamped MANIKIN 25 and inside lays a bed of double-sided tape. Her lead plate is stuck to the tape and the mould-tray is complete. Silicone is poured from a five-kilo tub into a beaker on a digital scale. The weight determines the amount of curative to add. It is vital to remove any trapped air bubbles, so Simon puts the beaker under a dome on something called a Vacu Cast machine that sucks out the air. He is careful to paint the first layer of silicone on the lead plate to ensure it is put down smoothly, then he pours silicone in the box to the rim. Any remaining bubbles rise to the surface where they are burst with the tip of a scalpel. While the silicone sets he slips into confessional mode. As he has hinted, there are problems. Pia's impression is that most stem from the pressures of too much work. He just can't keep pace with orders, many of which have been paid for in advance, and as a result has many unhappy customers.

'Could you take on an apprentice?'

He frowns. From Simon's perspective an apprenticeship means training someone who will eventually compete with him. While this is a logical concern the present danger is that those willing to pay for high-quality workmanship might turn in desperation to less accurate, cheaper and more reliable manufacturers elsewhere in the world. He turns the cigar box over and a slab of silicone drops out. The imprint of the leaf is bright white and details are hard to see until Simon paints the surface with Tiranti's Natural Copper Bronze Dusting Powder to make it conductive. He cuts two lengths of insulated copper wire, strips the ends, then inserts each wire in the mould. The other ends are shaped to hooks and the contraption is lowered in a copper sulphate bath in the corner of the electroforming bench. Two large blocks of copper are hung on the cathode rail and lowered in the solution. The plate will not be finished today but there will be something worth seeing. Given the drift of their conversation the decision to leave the plate might seem eccentric – but they have got on pretty well, Simon knows what he is doing, Pia is desperate for a piece of copper that she can print from and at this time the final outcome of James's experiments is unknown. The proposition takes Simon by surprise and he takes time to consider before agreeing on condition that costs, likely to be in the region of fifty pounds, are met in advance. The failure to read even this sign proves to Pia that she deserves what she gets. By the time they part a thin copper shell has formed on the bronze-painted area of the silicone, proving if nothing else that it is possible, even simple, for an expert craftsman to make a copper plate.

Several nature-printers including Auer experimented with gutta-percha – latex from the sap of a Malay tree, *Palaquium gutta*. Auer noted objects 'that by their form or fragility cannot be exposed to pressure against harder metals…are by us managed with a gutta-percha cover'. This substance was new to everyone in the West in 1843, when its useful properties were revealed by a colonial doctor called William Montgomerie.

Soon gutta-percha was insulating transatlantic telegraph cables. Dentists began to work with it for root canal obturation and it is still used today as a core filler material. Gutta-percha also transforms the popularity of golf. Until the 1840s golf balls were feathers in a leather case, expensive and useless in wet weather. Reverend Paterson of Dundee moulds a golf ball from gutta-percha and within five years the 'gutty' has become the ball of choice. At the Great Exhibition the newly formed Gutta-Percha Company presents a range of moulded furniture and engages in the production of all kinds of things, from boot-soles to picture frames, from 'unbreakable' vases to realistic deer-heads. It is even used to glue together sections of Bradbury's *The Nature-Printed British Ferns* in an early effort at that grand misnomer, perfect binding. It seems gutta-percha is the answer to every problem except there are not enough trees to meet the exponential increase in demand, so the market collapses.

English claims to the discovery of nature-printing rest on the work of a Sheffield doctor called Ferguson Branson who, in or around 1847, took nature-prints directly from gutta-percha; an idea no more improbable than that of gutta-percha golf balls, though there is something fantastic in the reckless confidence that encourages people to try things. The days are long in Victorian Britain that allow time for such blue-sky thinking. Branson follows through methodically on his hunch with a series of experiments conducted so carefully that he is able to present his findings to a learned body. At this time it seems anyone can be a scientist. Branson finds it impossible to make a clean impression but continues to experiment and realises that if he dusts the gutta-percha with bronze powder, then he can use his home-electrotyping kit to make a copper printing plate.

If a supplier can be found, gutta-percha might still be of use for nature-printing. The gum, which hardens in air, becomes soft when warmed gently to around 70°c, then retains its shape as it cools. This means that details impressed in the softened material are not lost as it hardens, so it *is* like the silicone Pia saw at Leeds and it could prove a viable alternative to lead for taking an impression.

Branson found electrotyping tiresome, discovered that brass and Britannia metal gave better results. He even experimented with transferring an image taken from the plate to a lithographic stone. Branson never made a serious attempt to develop the process further. There are a few rather ordinary prints at Sheffield City Museum. That's all. Not much is known of Branson beyond the fact that he was a painter, naturalist and one-time president of the Literary and Philosophical Society of Sheffield who delivered lectures on Shakespeare, Chaucer, on the Poetry of Form; and also on nature-printing.

* * *

It feels necessary to take a break from galvanoplastics. On a distracted afternoon at the V&A, when a discordant note is struck by parents struggling to control wayward children in the quadrangle, Pia comes across a pocket-size book by 'A.M.C' concerned with the troublesome task of collecting 'floating flowers' (butterflies). Pinning lepidoptera in a hermetically sealed box is fiddly and inconvenient. They can't be skinned like birds, pickled like snakes or pressed like flowers. What is a Victorian naturalist to do? The solution is a form of nature-printing in which butterflies are used like transfers, pressed on paper prepared with adhesive, then peeled off. French missionaries in India smeared paper with a mixture of honey, gum arabic and a little salt. Alas, directions for this mixture were too vague to admit of a good result. Experiments with other substances like wax and rice water proved inadequate for green and blue butterflies whose peculiar iridescence, the result of the grooving of their scales, was lost. Fortunately, the author's 'colloido-gelatine' process solves all the difficulties and:

> allows the collector to form his collection and carry it about in about as small a space as would be occupied by drawings of the same objects, whilst the accuracy of every line and mark, the delicacy of the shading, the brilliancy of the hues and the metallic sheen which appears on the wings of many of the tribe, is at the same time reproduced and preserved to a degree which is impossible in even the most carefully drawn and highly finished painting.

The primary concern here is aesthetic rather than scientific but over the road in the Natural History Museum are loose sheets between green boards containing nature-prints of *European Butterflies and a few Moths* collected, mounted and presented to Richard and Caroline Owen by Arthur Farre, MD. Sir Richard Owen is the driving force behind the establishment of the Natural History Museum in 1881.

Most of the colours of the wings are undimmed. There are many shades of brown, cream, yellow, some reds, strong oranges on *Vanessa urticae* (small tortoiseshell), flashes of blue on *Papilio machaon* (old world swallowtail), green on *Thecla rubi* (green hairstreak), and also faint purples and golds. Bodies have been retouched in watercolour, highlights added and legs and antennae painted in. As far as she can make out, four hundred and fifty-six creatures were harmed in the making of this remarkable work, 'the fruits of a physician's holiday in August 1855'.

At the Kunstbibliotek attached to the Royal Danish Academy of Fine Arts is a slim folder quarter-bound in red cloth with mottled brown boards, faded ties and the title PL Kyhl, Naturtryk (Nature-Printer). Inside are various papers and a thin dark green book with stiff card covers. This is *Description (with 46 drawings) of a method to copy flat objects of nature and art* dated Copenhagen, 1 May 1833. Title page and text are handwritten in a beautiful flowing script. The notes provide details of an approach that show the goldsmith to be meticulous and thoughtful. For instance, where he describes drying leaves between two sheets strewn with sand, left under a weight. For Kyhl, once is not enough:

Take the leaf out with due precaution, put it for a quarter of an hour into water and have it dried again as formerly, thus repeating this manipulation four or five times. By this I always found that the leaves gained in tenacity and firmness, lose their watery parts and become the more fit to be stamped.

The prints are the size of playing cards, monochrome, the subjects predictable – leaves, lace, feathers – and are of a quality that might have surprised Auer. It is interesting that Kyhl, who was not by trade a printer, tests two kinds of printing and both are successful. The usual intaglio image delivers a positive result. That is to say, the details are inked and the background is white. Occasionally, Kyhl gives us the same object in reverse. Like a negative, where only the background is inked. He explains:

the first leaves with their veins black and sunken are copper-prints, but the leaves with their body dark and veins light-coloured are zinc-prints or reversed prints from the original copper-plates.

The Staatsdruckerei in Vienna claimed to use relief printing for lace and obtained similar results. Few technical details are available about how the prints were made. In intaglio, only the marks below the surface of the plate are inked. The paper is forced into the plate, so the image is embossed – inked areas are raised above the surface of the paper. In relief, the surface is inked, the plate is impressed in the paper and the image appears debossed – inked areas are indented in the paper. In both cases the image is positive. With these Kyhl prints – and also with the lace prints from Vienna and the earlier ones from Nottingham – the image is negative (ie, the background only is inked) and it is embossed. Non-printed areas sit proud of the inked background and form the details of the image; like white lace on a deep blue bed. As far as Pia can judge, the only way to achieve this result with a relief press is by using a plate that has been prepared for intaglio printing. In this instance the inked *surface* of the intaglio plate forms the background of the image that is pushed in the paper by the relief press, leaving un-inked areas above the surface to form the details of the image. This may not be the correct explanation. Staring at such work is to be aware of technical limitations. There appears no way to achieve this result using an intaglio machine and yet Kyhl most likely used a goldsmith's rolling press. The closest she ever gets is when she places an inked leaf and a sheet of paper on an inked plate of copper and runs both through the press, with predictable results; a black-veined leaf on a black background. Peel the leaf off the plate and a ghostly image remains offset on the plate. If another sheet is laid on the plate and run through the press the result is a little like the Kyhl print, with flat white veins on grey.

In the folder is an article from *Philobiblon* published in 1930 in Vienna and another from *Archiv für Buchgewerbe* dated May 1908. Both are general reviews of the history of nature-printing and as usual Kyhl gets an honourable mention. There is also something unexpected. A wafer of metal foil the size of a coaster, silver on one side with gold on the other that is peeling and cracked. On the surface is a faint, slightly raised image of a leaf that does resemble closely one of the prints in the book. Could this possibly be one of Kyhl's plates? As a plate it seems too thin, but can there be any other explanation?

Kyhl's collected works in the Royal Academy occupy about the same shelf-space as a medium-size hardback novel, but there is another item at the nearby Design Museum, just across the cobbled square of Kongens Nytorv: a single volume in landscape format that, so far as she is aware, is not referred to in any accounts of Kyhl. It is not a published book in the usual sense of the word but rather a small collection of items bound between blue-and-grey marbled boards. Again, the name P L Kyhl in gothic lettering stamped in gold close to the top-left corner and a printed title page, *True Images of Natural Objects Printed From Those Objects*. On several pages, more of the same close-cropped nature-prints are pasted in like pictures in a scrapbook. As with most of his nature-printed work the emphasis is on the process rather than the composition. There is also a two-page A5 sheet printed letterpress with ornamental borders, an early example of a promotional flyer dated 1834 that is nothing less than a loud appeal for subscribers. There is even a form to be completed. Kyhl has more than a dilettante's interest in nature-printing and this is his attempt to rouse popular interest in his invention. There is no evidence further prints were ever made and presumably he decided to drop the scheme.

Kyhl appears in accounts of nature-printing because Auer chose to publish the details of Professor's Thiele's claims, and Bradbury ran with the story. It occurs to Pia that neither actually inspected much of Kyhl's work. Her suspicion is that hardly anyone else has seen it, either.

The short-lived ambition to show things as they are – liberated from the skill, imagination and invention of illustrators and engravers – is still a few years away, so for Kyhl it was a case of right idea, wrong time. In a few decades certain disciplines benefit from the pursuit of the uncontaminated image. British physicist Arthur Worthington uses freeze-frame photography to disprove his own long-held belief in the symmetrical form of splashes made by droplets of liquid falling on a horizontal plate. Gustav Hellman employs photomicographer Richard Neuhauss to demonstrate that the geometrical perfection of snowflakes is a myth.

But even in Auer's time, the case for the objective image was never fully accepted by botanists. For most purposes – and particularly when it came to identification – an illustration of the typical form of a plant was, as Hooker knew, more useful than a specific example that was likely to be unrepresentative. It's another reason why nature-printing failed to catch on. The determination of the age to persist with mechanical objectivity brings to mind a very short Borges' story, *On Exactitude in Science*, in which an empire obsessed with cartographic accuracy decides that only a map on the same scale as the empire will suffice.

The following Generations, who were not so fond of the Study of Cartography as their Forebears had been, saw that that vast map was Useless, and not without some Pitilessness was it, that they delivered it up to the Inclemencies of Sun and Winters. In the Deserts of the West, still today, there are Tattered Ruins of that Map, inhabited by Animals and Beggars; in all the Land there is no other Relic of the Disciplines of Geography.

Even so. Pia likes Kyhl's work and it's sad to reflect that things might have been different if only the thought had occurred to him a bit later, or if he had lived a little longer. As it is, his major accomplishment is to be given a lukewarm acknowledgement in a posthumous debate[1]. That Kyhl's short-lived experiment failed to attract much attention and was allowed to fall into obscurity feels unsatisfactory. What remains is an insignificant bundle of papers from a goldsmith, an outsider, someone with limited experience of printing or publishing and unattached to any academic institution; without either the means or the conviction to pursue his discovery. Premature ideas born in obscurity tend not to thrive and as no-one picked up on his achievement it amounts to little more than an intellectual dead end. In spite of suggestions from various English sources to the effect that the Viennese 'borrowed' from Kyhl, the chances of anyone outside Copenhagen knowing of his activity are surely too small to be taken seriously.

---

1 This is not an unusual occurrence. A contemporary example: years before Charles Darwin or Alfred Russel Wallace, Patrick Matthew proposed a version of the theory of evolution by natural selection – in the appendix to a book on naval timber.

Pia collects plants close to her family home in Småland. This area of Sweden is the birthplace of naturalist Carl Linnaeus, who visited England several times to meet renowned gardener Philip Miller at Chelsea Physic Garden. Miller thought Linnaeus conceited but eventually accepted his system of binomial nomenclature, with some reservations, for the eighth edition of his *Gardeners Dictionary*. The two men were also connected by Georg Dionysius Ehret, one of the finest of Eighteenth Century botanical illustrators. Linnaeus met Ehret in Holland. A little later Ehret went to England where he married Susanna Kennet, the sister of Philip Miller's wife. Ehret contributed to Miller's *Gardeners Dictionary* and provided illustrations for *Figures of Plants*. The Garden can thus lay claim to a long tradition of botanical illustration. Perhaps the most well-known of its artists is 'heroic' Elizabeth Blackwell, whose hapless husband Alexander landed in a debtors' prison, leaving her to figure out how to live and keep her child. She saw a gap in the market for a new herbal, took rooms next to the Physic Garden at 4, Swan Walk – and it was here that she began drawing the plants from life, engraving the copper plates and finally, hand-colouring each of the printed images. Isaac Rand, Demonstrator of Plants at the Garden, is full of encouragement, as is noted doctor Richard Mead; and Sir Hans Sloane. They all recognise the need for an illustrated herbal, as there are so many new plants in the Garden from all over the world. With Joseph Miller's consent Elizabeth cribs detail from his *Botanicum Officinale*. (This book predates the nature-printing effort Pia presents to students.) Her husband helps with the text. From 1737 to 1739, she publishes four plates every week, each set accompanied by a hand-written page of introductions with locations, succinct descriptions and common uses of the plants:

Plate 360 The Scythian Lamb. *Agnus Scythicus*
1 This is a moss that grows upon the roots of a Fern,
of a light brown colour.
2 It grows in Tartary and Scythia.
3 It is esteem'd good for all kinds of Fluxes and
Haemorrhagies, and to stop the Bleeding of Green Wounds.
Latin, Borometz

Income from the magnum opus, *A Curious Herbal containing five hundred cuts of the most Useful Plants now used in the Practice of Physick*, secures the release of an unreformed husband. After failing at more ventures and incurring further debts Alexander leaves his family in 1742 for Sweden, of all places, where he gains and loses the post of court physician, then mismanages a model farm at Ållestad. Elizabeth sends him royalties from the herbal and is on her way to visit him when he loses his head. The details are sketchy and by all accounts the accusation of treason is a trumped-up charge. Blackwell even manages to mess up his own execution, laying his head face-up on the block. When this mistake is pointed out he apologises, explaining that this is his first beheading; it will not happen again.

Like many members of the Florilegium Society, Gillian Barlow thinks the work of Elizabeth Blackwell less exciting than her life. There is, for example, a picture of an orange tree in which an orange depends from a branch at an unnatural angle. The fact that Blackwell's handiwork is given prominence in the context of the Garden is a matter of dissatisfaction for some, because the exacting discipline of botanical illustration today transcends even photography in meeting the precise requirements of science; and occasionally the observed details reveal things missed by botanists. And it is not only a question of accuracy. Artifice underpins the composition of any subject. Gillian will suspend tiny weights from stems to achieve the desired effect. There is real skill in this and much to be learned, which accounts for the success of Florilegium Society courses and also for any reservations it may harbour over Elizabeth Blackwell's heritage status.

Arranging plants is also an exacting task for Pia. Each is fixed with great care on site as soon as it is collected; the positions of stems, leaves and roots are secured with archival tape on acid-free paper and pressed between boards. The pressing is of particular significance for nature-printing, since it goes some way to determining the aesthetic qualities of the image.

In addition to her collection, Pia owns a single herbarium inherited from a friend's mother: yellowed foolscap pages, bone-white stalks of grasses with dusty seed-heads sewn in position with linen thread. It seems a relic, memorial to a time when it was acceptable to gather wild flowers. And surprising and beautiful examples of herbariums survive, like the one made by Emily Dickinson (viewable online[1]) and the many examples at Kew. Towards the close of the 19th Century, sparked by the embers of the fern craze, there was a fad for gathering, drying and mounting specimens of ferns in albums. Many were compiled in New Zealand and sent back to relatives and friends in the old country. Most came from Auckland and Dunedin. Michael Hayward, a collector and member of the Fern Society, owns examples from Australia, India, Germany, England and Wales that can be seen in an online gallery (fernalbums.co.uk). On display there are various herbaria and other oddities, such as Jamaican fern doilys and lacebark fern fans sold for the benefit of the orphanage for girls in Kingston. In useful albums specimens are labelled and have been assembled by professionals between engraved kauri wood or parquetry covers. One or two of the unlabelled and anonymous albums contain beautiful arrangements. Only rarely is there any printed text but *Patinson's Gleanings Among the British Ferns* by Jane M Patinson

1 http://pds.lib.harvard.edu/pds/view/4184689

published in 1858 includes descriptive notes and, towards the
end, fifty lines of remorseless 'poetical composition' including:

Ye love to rear your feathery stems, the wandering winds to woo
And bathe before the flowers have woke, in morning's clearest dew!

Dens Leonis. Dandelion.

Above and overleaf: Joseph Miller, Demonstrator at Chelsea Physic Garden (1740-48) and Praefectus Horti (1743-47) created a unique record of the Garden with hand-coloured prints taken directly from individual specimens of plants in the two-volume *Icones Plantarum officinalium*. One volume focuses on medicinal plants and the other on species introduced recently to the country. See p5.

s *Veneris verus.* The true Mai

Plate 138.

Hart's Tongue.

1. Seed.

Lingua Cervina. & Phyllitis.

E: Blackwell delin. sculp. et Pinx.

A botanical illustration from *A Curious Herbal* (1737-39) by Elizabeth Blackwell, a contemporary of Joseph Miller. Information from another of Miller's works, *Botanicum officinale*, was lifted 'with his Consent' by Elizabeth Blackwell to add credibility to the text. See p123.

ONAGRACEÆ. (*Juss*)
Epilobium angustifolium L.
ROSE - BAY WILLOW - HERB.

Nature Printing.

PRINTED IN COLOURS BY
BRADBURY & EVANS WHITEFRIARS, LONDON.

Nature-prints from Henry Bradbury's first work, published in 1854, are shown here and overleaf. The full title is: *A Few Leaves Represented by "Nature-Printing" Showing the Application of the Art for the Reproduction of Botanical and Other Natural Objects with a Delicacy of Detail and Truthfulness Unobtainable by Any Other Known Method of Printing.* See p96.

ROSACEÆ. *(Juss)*

Spiræa Ulmaria. L

MEADOW SWEET.

According to *The Examiner*, 'A number of well-known plants – ferns, celandine, the yellow pimpernel, tormentilla, nettle, the hedge woundwort, meadow-sweet, &c – are here printed off from fresh and well-chosen specimens, so accurately as to give the character of foliage and the general appearance of the flower, with as much truth as there could be in the dried specimen, and with more beauty.' The 'see-through' quality of these images must have seemed extraordinary to contemporaries, especially as X-rays were not discovered until another forty-one years had passed.

A. Ceterach officinarum.
B. Gymnogramma leptophylla. C. Blechnum Spicant.

NATURE PRINTING.

Plates from *The Ferns of Great Britain and Ireland Nature-Printed by Henry Bradbury* (1855-6) are shown here and overleaf. Plants used for printing were provided by collectors from all over the country. The source of each specimen used for printing is acknowledged (the location and the collector) as part of the explanation of each plate. For example, one specimen of *Ceterach offininarum* (*Asplenium ceterach*) was found in Bath by the Rev E Bosanquet. Another was discovered in North Lancashire by Miss S Beever.

Seventeen facsicles of Bradbury's first monumental work on ferns (each page is 560x370mm) were offered from June 1855 to September 1856 at six shillings each; and the volume for an eye-watering six guineas. In 1855, according to Roderick Cave, this represented half of the annual income of a cook. Nature-prints are still extremely valuable. At the time of writing a single copy of *The Ferns of Great Britain and Ireland* is available for sale from Arader Galleries in New York for just over £10,000.

The Nature-Printed British Sea-Weeds (1859-1860) was the last to be printed by Henry Bradbury. A pamphlet promoting the work begins: 'The Art of Nature-Printing is now so well known and appreciated in this country, through the publication of *The Ferns of Great Britain and Ireland,* that it is needless here to recapitulate the many advantages it has over engraving, however well executed: and in no department of Botany can we expect to see it so truthfully and beautifully carried out as in our Algae.' Following Bradbury's death, a number of planned works were shelved. See p156.

View to St Stephan's Cathedral from the k. k. Hof- und Staatsdruckerei zu Wien (The Imperial Printing Office, Vienna) circa 1852. An albumen print (365x267mm) by Georg J Hackel, director of the photography department. Auer believed 'the entire world should be gradually reproduced in pictures'. As the inks fade, dark marks reveal where the photograph had been retouched. See p138.

Naturselbstdruck.

A plate from Auer's *Die Entdeckung Des Naturselbstdruckes oder Die Erfindung*, published in Vienna in 1853. The full title in English is: *The Discovery of the Natural Printing-Process. An invention for creating by means of the Original itself – in a swift and simple manner – plates for printing copies of Plants, Materials, Lace, Embroideries, Originals, or Copies, containing the most delicate profundities or elevations as not to be detected by the human eye – which plates for printing are capable of producing two results on paper – the one producing a copy of the original, upon a white ground, in various colours with one single impression – the other producing a copy in white upon a coloured ground – the latter by the ordinary Letterpress – the former by the Copper-plate press – in both instances without the aid of drawing or engraving.*

Blatt.
Aronia rotundifolia.

Mose
Mnium undulatum

Algen
Echinoceras pellucidum Kz

stdruck.

er Fisch

Holzdurchschnitt.
Saphora japonica *L.*

Achat.

Blatt
Bauhinia speciosa.

Spitzen.

Naturselbstdruck.

Aus der k. k. Hof- und Staatsdruckerei zu Wien. 1853.

Blätter des Manns Waldfarn.
(Polystichum Filix mas. Roth.)

Two images from Auer's *Die Entdeckung Des Naturselbstdruckes oder Die Erfindung*, including prints of leaves that incredulous botanists believed so true to nature as to be indistinguishable from the objects themselves. Previous page: the showcase composite published in 1857 in the magazine *Kosmos* (similar versions appeared in *Faust* and *Gutenberg*) demonstrates a broad range of applications of nature-printing undertaken by the Staatsdruckerei: a snakeskin, a fossilised fish, agate, lace, moss, seaweed, leaves, the end-grain of wood; and a bat.

Each thread is visible in the remarkable prints of lace that appeared in *Die Entdeckung*. Members of the Austrian chamber of commerce 'found the resemblance so deceptive, that they took them to be real lace'. Opposite: 'Professor von Perger made further application of this idea for ornamental drawings, and at his instigation the director of the academy of sciences, Mr Ruben, sent... several sorts of plants, twisted in the form of a wreath, the copies of which produced ecstasy.' (*Die Entdeckung*.)

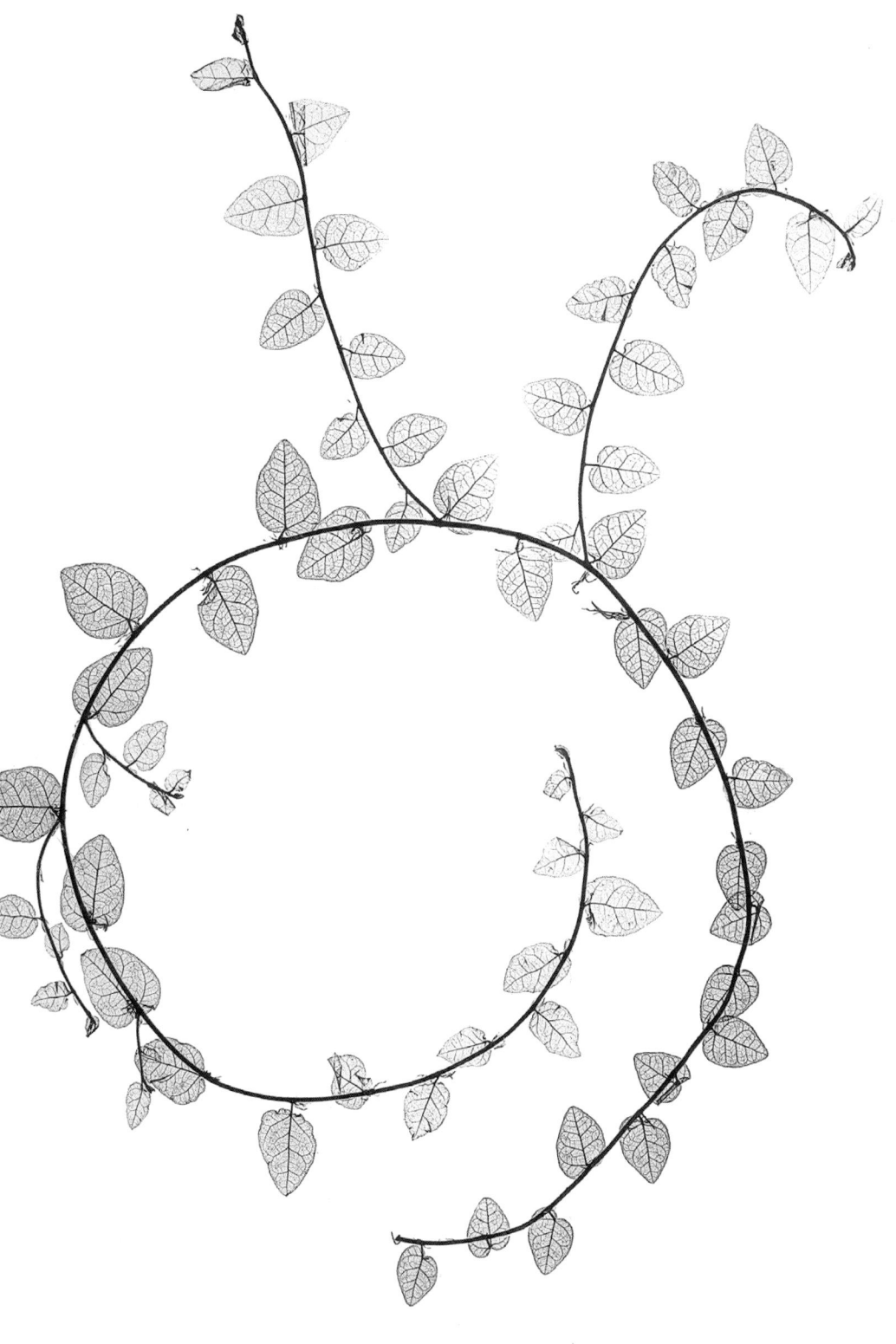

Ranke vom kletternden Feigenstrauch.
(Ficus stipulata. Thnb.)

Photograph © Michael Hayward

A typical nature-print from *Physiotypia plantarum austriacarum* (1856-73) by Constantin Freiherrn von Ettingshausen and Dr Alois Pokorny. The single colour used for all prints gave them the appearance of desiccated herbarium specimens. The full size of this image is 580x410mm. See p136.

Opposite: detail of an original copper plate from the Staatsdruckerei formed from an imprint in lead. The image on the plate is raised. A separate plate must be made to create a recessed image suitable for intaglio printing. See p135.

Examples of the pioneering nature-prints of Peter Khyl from the 1830s which appeared in a small pamphlet, *Tro afbildninger af natur-gjenstande frembragte ved aftruk af Gjenstandene selv*. Auer denied knowledge of Khyl's work, explaining that even 'in the capital of Denmark, everybody was ignorant of its existence'. It appears that Khyl's attempts to find subscribers for 'True representations of natural objects produced directly from those objects' did not meet with success. See p118.

A monoprint of *Plantago major* made by Pia Östlund, inspired by the work of Peter Kyhl. See images on previous page.

A study of Pia's workspace at Arcane Studios in East London. Pinned to the wall is a sheet of notes from her visit to Leeds. See p107.

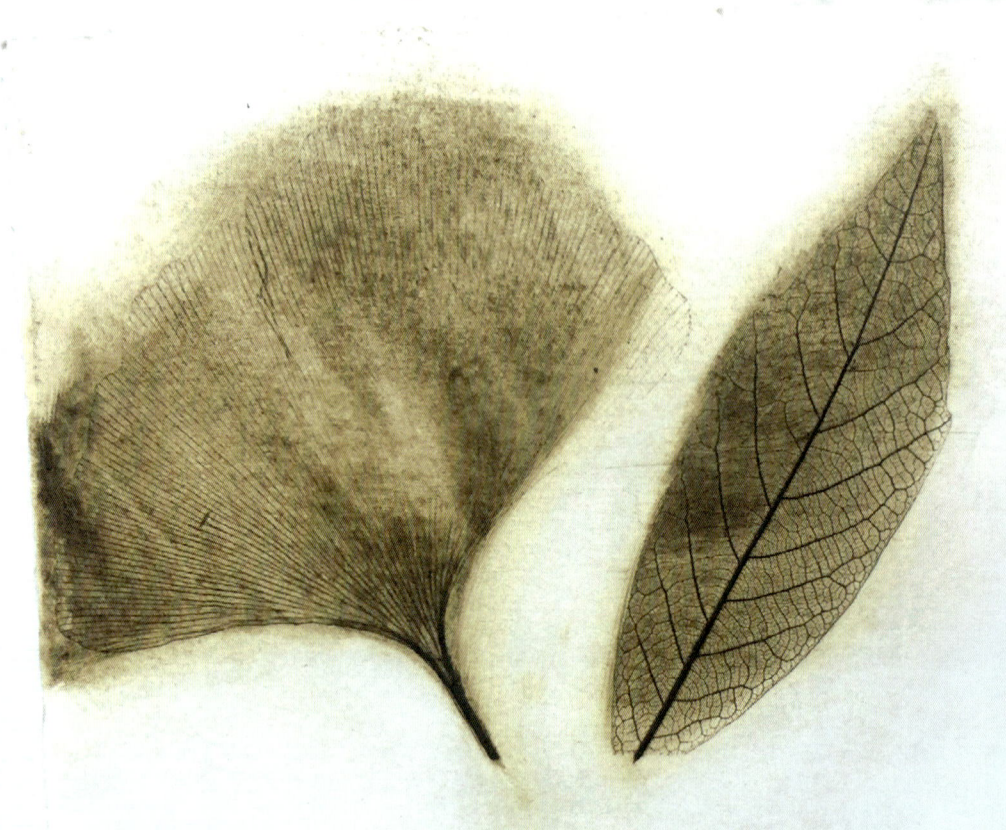

3 LP5

Examples of Pia's early struggles, including an image of the ill-fated gingko leaf. See p51.

The four stages in the preparation of a lead plate (clockwise from the top-left). Dried plant; polished lead plate; plant in position; impression of plant in lead. The copper-plate taken from the lead can be seen in the picture of Pia's studio. Opposite: lifting a nature-print from the plate. Overleaf: nature-print of an oak leaf by Pia Östlund.

The distinguished figure of Michael Hayward is waiting for Pia outside a small station in the shadow of Liverpool. She arrives on time and they drive through quiet residential streets to a comfortable family home that has shaped itself to accommodate his interests. Michael is a collector of nature-prints and has given her permission to inspect his library.

Before they begin, she is shown a small studio that Michael has set up to photograph the nature-prints of Colonel Jones for a special publication due for release shortly by the British Pteridological Society. Arthur Mowbray Jones, founder member of the Society, offered a limited edition of close on three hundred prints of ferns unbound in batches between 1876 and 1880. Like the prints in Joseph Miller's book at the Physic Garden these are taken directly from the plants. Pia examines several sheets. The prints are clean and sharp in black ink, with the stalks impressed heavily in the paper. They are a solid historical record of the preferences of Victorian fern collectors but to her eye they are not beautiful. Why did Jones choose not to use the more sophisticated techniques of Auer and Bradbury? Michael shrugs and points out that the last book to use what he calls the 'lead plate process' was published in 1873. It is sobering to think that the golden age of nature-printing lasted only twenty years.

'It is time-consuming, expensive and from a botanical point of view there are weaknesses. The colours are occasionally inaccurate. The detail of venation is wonderful, but the trade-off is unreal surface transparency.' That Michael of all people should voice such criticisms is remarkable. After all he is one of the few to own nearly all of the works of Bradbury and Auer. 'Also, as you are finding out, it is difficult. No-one has made nature-prints this way in Britain since the time of Henry Bradbury.' In the living room, the walls creak with outsize antiquarian tomes. Michael slips out to fire-up the coffee machine, returns with cake and expresso and Pia senses, not for the first time, how kind it is of him to allow her to intrude. He ushers her to a comfortable chair and asks where she'd like to begin. Anywhere. As he brings over the first volume she asks what he likes about 'lead plate' prints. 'Oh, they are a sublime mystery, like ferns. And they possess a certain other-worldly beauty, I suppose. They're not necessarily *my* favourite nature-prints, but it was Bradbury's monumental work on ferns that hooked me.'

They puzzle over other matters, such as Auer's claim that an audience presented with his printed leaves could not at first distinguish them from real leaves. It seems a childish prank and he suggests those early prints were made from a lead plate, then cut out to remove grubby marks that would have been inevitable on the edges of the image.

Over the next few hours a procession of extraordinary books of staggering significance parades before her eyes. Several do not exist in any British library and there is covetous pleasure to be had in handling them. Many are extremely valuable. A much later edition in very poor condition of one book, *Botanica in originali pharmaceutica*, went for £20,000 at auction in London some years ago. Very few copies of this edition exist. A New York dealer offered an identical set recently for sale and described it as unique. Printed in 1733 in Erfurt, it was the first book to use nature-printing as the primary mode of illustration and is one of Michael's favourites. Kniphof's hand-coloured prints are jewels but in spite of its importance, Pia is not entirely convinced. The frontispiece is good but throughout the flowers are often flat blocks of colour with no definition on petals and there are clumsily hand-painted details. The printing is uneven, too, as far as she can make out. Michael has other extremely rare volumes containing the artwork of Johann Hieronymous Kniphof. Hardly surprising as it appears he has just about everything ever produced on the subject of nature-printing other than the notebook in which Leonardo da Vinci offered directions on how to print directly from leaves; and oh, anything by Peter Kyhl. Most involve a different line of nature-printing than the one in which she is interested but there is much to marvel at. For example, the effort of Henry Smith (supervisor of the government printing press in Madras) called *Specimens of Nature-Printing from Unprepared Plants*, published in 1851. For direct prints these are remarkably sharp and detailed. Sometimes two sides of the same arrangement face each other across a single spread. The first prints are black but after a while Smith experiments with colour. The results are mixed, which encourages the reader to make comparisons. And the final print in the book is a snake captured in a graceful moment of lateral undulation.

Michael thinks Pia should offer a set of nature-printed ferns to subscribers through the Fern Society. It feels like a good, if premature, proposal. For him the promise of Pia's work proves a collection is never complete which, in turn, suggests collecting is a form of desperation; the need to need something, stretching for that which remains tantalisingly out of reach. By the end of the day Pia has exhausted all terms of admiration. There is just one more question. 'And if you had to choose one book?' She expects Michael to refer to something seen already but, to her rising horror, he searches a different set of shelves and pulls out a three-volume set of James Edward Smith's *Flora Britannica* with nature-printed marginalia on more than two hundred pages, small prints of flowers and leaves made in lampblack and hand-coloured by Susanna Walcott sometime around 1819. It is, she must agree, yet another very beautiful object and also one to which it is impossible to apply any focus. On the train home a spinning headache rushes upon her like a long dark tunnel. Her own fault for attempting to look at everything when there was simply too much to see.

Like the house in Northwood Hills, Caroline's small but luxuriant garden backs on to a railway line. In a lean-to off the kitchen are rows of sealed plastic bags. Each contains a labelled pot.

'The Fern Society's spore exchange,' she explains. 'A simple cheap way to obtain species.'

Cost-effective it may be, simple it is not. She unfolds a small foil tab to reveal a brown smudge that might be dust or a Class A substance. Hard to believe that it amounts to anything and easy to see why such plants are known as cryptogams. The absence of seeds ensured the reproduction of ferns remained for many years a mystery to gardeners. Caroline is happy to reveal the secrets and fortunately all stages of development are to hand in her lean-to. Here is a tray of sterilised soil that has been sowed with spores. It looks like soil. And over here is a tray that is is carpeted with what looks like green algae.

'Are these ferns?'

'No, not really. Each prothallus is a haploid gametophyte.'

Of course it is. Then again, if Pia was a botanist she would not have asked the question. Caroline tries again. Each of the tiny heart-shaped forms has a single set of chromosomes and develops both male and female parts. She points at a tray containing a large number of small ferns and says:

'A botanist will tell you a diploid sporophyte emerges from the zygote and is attached initially to the gametophyte but soon over-whelms it with roots, rhizomes and leaves.'

'So a fern exists in two different plant forms in its life?'

'Yes, a fertilised egg endowed with a full set of chromosomes becomes a fern that engulfs the parent plant.'

One of the more obvious challenges for someone aiming to replicate the work of Bradbury concerns the size of ferns. While it is not always the case, many mature ferns have sizeable fronds and these would require large plates – an expensive proposition. Caroline's idea is to offer Pia one-year and two-year sporelings, some of which are still only a few centimetres high. The propagation of these unassuming plants is a slow business.

'You'll be doing me a favour,' says Caroline. The shelves in the small room are crammed with pots and it is clear that she has many more plants than could be accommodated in her garden. Most are given away (the Fern Society also organises a plant exchange programme for sporelings) and Pia is added to the list of recipients. Caroline also donates pressed leaves from a Wild Service tree. It proved impossible to obtain 'ancient woodland' status in time to protect from development the land on which it grows and she would like a souvenir print.

There were no plans to pursue Bradbury or Auer any further than necessary to reach an understanding of the nature-printing process. All the same, boarding her budget flight to Vienna, Pia experiences a rush of anticipation that makes her wonder about Bradbury. After all, she is following in his purposeful steps. What was he thinking as he left the country for the most prestigious printing-house in the world?

Doubtless he had a secure position in the family firm. Bradbury & Evans was a reputable printer and publisher with a strong list (Wilkie Collins, William Thackeray, Anthony Trollope and Charles Dickens, among others) and at twenty-two he may have been a confident, assured young man; but surely Henry Bradbury must have felt a sense of nervous excitement as he set off to unearth the arcana of the Staatsdruckerei and to meet its director, Alois Auer, imperial government counsellor, director of the imperial Court and Government printing office, knight of the imperial Austrian order of the iron crown third class and of Francis-Joseph, of the papal Gregory order, of the Brasilian order of the rose, of the order of the Zähringer lion of the grand-duke of Baden, of the Louis order first class of the grand-duke of Hesse, proprietor of the Austrian large golden medal for art and science, actual member of the imperial academy of science at Vienna, of the German-Oriental society of Halle-Leipsic, of the Asiatic society at Paris, of the royal Asiatic society of Great Britain and Ireland at London, member of the Upper-Austrian trade-society and of the Museum Francisco-Carolinum for Austria above the river Enns and Salzburg, honorary member of the historical society for Carinthia, of the British academy of science, art and trade, and of the Ethnological society of London, then corresponding member of the royal academy of sciences and the fine arts at Modena.

The full title captures something of the weirdness of the Austrian Empire in which autodidactic Auer, a diminutive man of humble origins, served as a loyal subject. Was Henry Bradbury impressed, or did he set his shoulder against the bristling array of titles?

* * *

There are mitigating factors to account for the edgy thoughts whirling around Pia on the coach from the airport to the centre of Vienna. The future of her project rides on this short visit with its ambitious itinerary. Several bureaucratic hoops materialise late on and are jumped with difficulty. For example one of two institutes should grant permission to view the plates but it isn't clear to whom this honour falls, a situation that is not eased by the failure of the Museum of Natural History to respond to emails. Finally the permissions issue is resolved without its involvement, but she is still interested to see if there is any material at the museum and heads there first.

The grand building is deathly quiet, a fact accentuated by the quantity of stuffed animals on display. Londoners have come to expect museums to function as tourist traps and glorified playgrounds. The stillness here is unnerving. A quick circuit yields nothing more than the disapproving glare of a shoebill. At this point she should return to the ticket office and explain herself. Being slightly hyper she decides to push on and does not hesitate even when confronted by a sign with a very clear instruction in English: No Entry. On the other side of the Staff Only entrance is a courtyard, a staircase and a long corridor of closed doors. She wanders past various departments and gets precise directions from an unquestioning employee to an office where she meets Johanna, PA to the Head of Archives (who is on sabbatical). From a shelf behind her head Johanna plucks a publication written by her boss in 2003 about *Der Naturselbstdruck, a Viennese Invention*. While Pia browses the leaflet Johanna remembers there is a small exhibition in the museum on the very subject. They walk into the public space past the shoebill to the top of a staircase Pia has not climbed and, in an atrium outside the main exhibition hall, come face-to-face with carefully composed information boards that provide a thorough introduction to the art of nature-printing. Here are prints of grasses from the *Physiotypia plantarum Austriacarum* of Ettingshausen and Pokorny. And here is a salt print of Alois Auer von Welsbach with his family taken in 1859, when things were still going well for him. Looking at the board Johanna is reminded suddenly of something else and in hushed tones tells how the museum, in connection with its centenary celebrations a few years ago, borrowed one of the Staatsdruckerei plates from the Botanical Institute and attempted to make a new print from it. As Pia turns Johanna raises a hand to wave away her obvious excitement. She can't remember the details.

'To be honest,' she whispers, 'I don't think it turned out so good.'

They shake hands and Johanna leaves Pia to look at the boards and puzzle over how to raise the matter at her next appointment – at the Botanical Institute.

* * *

The Department of Botany and Biodiversity Research, part of the University of Vienna, is located in the third district, a thirty-minute trundle from the centre. Pia has brought along a tin of Fortnum & Mason biscuits to sweeten her reception and although the librarian, Robert Stangl, does not seem the type to be taken in by sugary blandishments, they result in crumbs of good feeling. Stangl explains that the Botanical Institute came by the plates after the first World War when the printing house, keen to dispose, passed them over for the cost of the copper. Since then, the plates have been kept in the storeroom. A desk nearby has been allocated to Pia and she waits while Andre Biot, the Assistant Librarian, goes to fetch a plate. It is placed carefully on the table in front of her and she feels like a gourmand presented with the best dish in a restaurant.

'Is this what you expected?' he asks.

In a way it is, but without seeing a plate it would have been hard to make one with any conviction. Now she knows what a plate should look like and realises why the so-called 'mother plate' is an essential step in the process.

What she is looking at is a beautiful piece of copper, about the size of an A3 sheet of paper, a little less than 2mm thick, with a number in the corner that probably relates to its position in the book. Any pits or imperfections on the reverse have been filled with lead, so it is very smooth on both sides. The raised image on the copper (taken from the lead) looks exactly like a pressed plant fixed in place – perfectly preserved and apparent, from the tip of tap root to fibrous stem, from midrib to the reticulate pattern of veins on leaf. Surprisingly, the plate has been retouched. Imperfections from the lead, specks of dust and all extraneous details have been removed from the non-image areas with a burnisher. This is highly skilled corrective work and it means that when the final printing plate is made, all of the glitches that are an inevitable part of working in lead will have been obliterated. This is not the same as altering the image and in fact, the image does not appear to have been changed. From a scientific perspective the virtue of nature-printing lies in its presentation of the bare unaccommodated plant; the thing itself, unadorned and untouched, an objective tamper-proof image. When Kyhl suggested in his short treatise that details might be improved with an etching needle Auer could not resist adding a prim exclamation mark. As if to say, who would ever countenance such a thing? Auer claimed of his own work that copies were 'obtained by means of the original itself without the aid of a designer, engraver or any other artist'. Perhaps these days, when trust in the integrity of any picture is at an all-time low, the news that a printing-plate has been slightly improved is not news at all.

The plates in Vienna are from Constantin Freiherr von Ettingshausen's and Alois Pokorny's monumental twelve-elephant-folio, *Physiotypia plantarum Austriacarum*. The first volume was released in 1856 by the Staatsdruckerei under the directorship of Auer. It took seventeen years to produce the entire work and according to Roderick Cave later volumes were published elsewhere (by F Tempsky, of Prague). Ettingshausen, a paleobotanist, believed nature-prints provided the perfect means of comparing living plants with fossils. The paleobotanical output of Ettingshausen and Pokorny at the Staatsdruckerei is ascetic and of all nature-printed productions it takes the most rigorously scientific approach. A single colour was used for all specimens. In a work on such a grand scale this might have been a cost-saving exercise, especially as accountants were beginning to take an interest. More probably the use of a single colour was an attempt to remove a variable. The artistic – and therefore subjective – use of colour might have detracted from the fine exactitude in representation of the structure of each plant. These prints mimic specimens of dried flowers and in producing a printed herbarium, the implication is that they are a perfect substitute for exsiccati. They have additional benefits: they don't deteriorate over time, they are not as fragile as dried plants; and from a single original it is possible to make a large number of duplicates.

More plates appear and by the end of the afternoon Pia is able to visit the backroom and help herself. She takes many photographs and makes notes. It is remarkable that so many of these obsolete objects have survived for so long. She remembers what Johanna at the Museum of Natural History said about making a new print from one of the plates. Andre scowls in a way that, oddly enough, brings to mind a shoebill.

'It's true. The Museum of Natural History wanted to make a keepsake for its anniversary. Something went wrong when they tried to make the printing-plate and the original was spoiled completely.'

'Did they try again?'

Andre shrugs his shoulders dismissively. The Botanical Institute is not dead set against utilising elements of its hoard but is reluctant to incur further losses. 'I think perhaps it is not quite as simple as it sounds,' he says with a gentle smile, as if he has been reading her thoughts. He takes a biscuit, walks to the window and changes the subject, pointing out that the printing office used to be next door and moved just after the war. There was bomb damage. The printing-office is now a private company and she has an appointment there, tomorrow. 'I can imagine botanists running back and forth with plants and nature-prints,' says Andre, looking out. He's being playful but is surprised when Pia points out that nature-printing had ceased long before they became neighbours. Andre is shocked and goes away to consult his archives. It's true. The original works, home to Auer and the curious nature-printing interlude, is at Singerstraße 26, in the heart of the city. This building survives, occupied now by a variety of businesses close to her hotel.

The large grey building is the Franziskaner Kirche St Hieronymous. Guide-books say the style is south German Renaissance, with obvious Baroque additions. It is in good shape. Pia is in the smart part of town. Adjoining the church is the home of the Imperial printing-house during Auer's tenure.

Hard to explain what draws her here, other than curiosity. Does she really expect to discover any trace of those times? Another stack of printing-plates? A box of fern prints in some neglected corner? A quick stroll round the block reveals a façade that is largely unchanged. The names on the wall-plaque beside the large green doors are new: konservatorium wien, privatuniversität. There are small retailers – an off licence, a florist, a picture gallery, an antiques shop. The building, following the line of earlier cloisters, is constructed around a quad-rangle (now a car-park, a token sign of the times). It is late afternoon. On impulse Pia pushes through the main door to a dreary hallway with the uncared-for feel of common parts of shared buildings everywhere: postboxes on one wall, a stack of chairs, a bicycle; and a flight of worn stone steps like an invitation.

One flight leads to another. She climbs them all. On each level are broad black doors made from iron panels that might be original features. There is a lively conversation between stringed instruments somewhere on the third floor but she doesn't see anyone until she reaches the architect's practice at the very top. A woman sitting at a desk rises to greet her and listens politely as Pia explains the reason for her interest in the building, describing its heritage with a great outrush of enthusiasm.

'You are telling me this building was the global centre of creative media in the Nineteenth Century?' You could put it like that. The woman is surprised and it is clear that her day has never been disturbed by the autocratic spirit of Auer, or any revenant printer's devil. There is nothing here now. It is just an office. But she is free to look around. Through the window is a magnificent view of St Stephan's cathedral. It is uncannily familiar and in a flash Pia realises that she has seen this *exact* view before; an albumen print in an issue of *Faust*, the magazine published by Auer's brother. The picture was taken on this very spot in about 1852 by Georg Hackel, who had just succeeded Pretsch as director of the department, as an illustration of the use of photography for landscapes. The objectives of photography were defined by Auer: for landscapes, for the reproduction of works of art, for the duplication of images and lastly, for the benefit of science (micro-photography – or photomicrography, as it is known now – was a speciality of the department). Strangely, Auer did not consider portraiture of public interest so it did not lie within the remit of the photographic department of the printing-office. If this seems short-sighted, the Great Exhibition jury shared the same opinion: photographs were 'unsurpassed for reproducing sculptural objects, or capturing views, or for enlarging or reducing paintings' and might 'serve as study pieces for the creative artist'.

'What is it? Have you seen a ghost?' The secretary is at her shoulder. Pia explains that one of the first photographs of Vienna – of anywhere, really – was taken right here, is framed by this window. Auer was impressed with the result and remarked 'who is in the position, and what means would be required, through the imitative organs – the eye and the hand – to convey all the millions of details?'.

* * *

The scene from the window in the architect's office is encouraging and provides the momentum, once back on the street, to push into the antiques shop in pursuit of that imaginary box of nature-prints. It's stuffy and unexpectedly busy. There is music from a radio, a little dog is yapping at a baby crying in a buggy. When Pia tries to explain herself to the proprietor she cannot make herself understood. Then there is a tap on her shoulder and half-turning she meets an elderly man wearing a grey Homburg, a wool coat, with an umbrella over his arm. Has he heard correctly? Is she interested in the Printing-office? When she begins to explain, he nods at the door. This is how she makes the acquaintance of Professor Schweizer who, by coincidence, is from Switzerland. As they stroll along Singerstraße towards St Stephan's conversation is easy. He studied at Cambridge, his specialism is plant genetics, he is very fond of Chelsea Physic Garden. His memories of the Garden that he has not visited for sixty years are revealing because they show it has not changed out of sight. This pleases him.

'Special places are easily lost. Sometimes it is better to leave things as they are. For example...' He ushers Pia in to Café Hawelka, which he says looks much the same as when it reopened, in 1945.

'Viennese coffee house culture is listed by UNESCO. What a good idea, to defend our "intangible cultural heritage" against the caprice of progress and those people who want to make their mark by "improving" things.'

He hands his coat, hat and umbrella to a waiter and they sit side by side on a red-and-yellow striped sofa. The Professor tells her he also started in Vienna in 1945, at the Botanic Institute. His first job was to clear the place up, because they had been 'bombed about a bit'. The phrase echoes the opening sequence of *The Third Man* and immediately it brings to mind the deep shadows and deserted streets of a damaged city and the haunted faces of desperate men on street corners captured by flawless off-kilter cinematography. She pictures the Professor in silhouette clambering over the rubble to buy a balloon on a string.

Coffees arrive while Pia explains why she is here. The Professor is familiar with nature-printing and knows about the plates at the Botanic Institute. With a wry smile he suggests that nature-printing was one of the more unusual notions to come out of the printing-office, though he concedes it says much about the imagination and enthusiasm of Auer. The way that Auer developed and promoted new processes is admirable.

For example, Auer commissioned a large work of natural history as soon as he realised that technical mastery of micro-photography was possible, even though a practical way of reproducing photographs in print had not been found, because he wanted to demonstrate the value of such images for science. He employed a research scientist to prepare plates and another specialist to write the text to support the work, an initiative that took most of a decade.

'You see the way he brings technology to science; it is a visionary approach.'

This example suggests Auer is due some credit for the achievements of the printing-office. He was the driving force. He was running the show. In an 1853 overview of the printing-office, photography and 'mikrotypie' (micro-photography) were listed as sections of the nature-printing department.

'There is one thing I can show you that concerns Auer, if you have the time, just a few minutes from here.' They walk slowly through the warm evening to the Austrian Academy of Sciences, Pia's cheeks aglow with a sense of her good fortune. Professor Schweizer is an elected member with a named peg for his hat and coat, a symbol of privilege more impressive than any gold card. She is admitted as his guest. A short tour of grand rooms follows, culminating at the Festival Hall.

'There is a fire in the 1960s and the ceiling collapses. The fresco you see here is a restoration. It's a good job and it proves things are seldom what they seem to be.'

'So this is where Auer gives his lectures?'

Only some of them, it seems. The Academy arrives here in 1857, occupying the former university building that closed in 1848 following the insurrection. Auer's pronouncements on nature-printing might have been delivered to an earlier incarnation of the Academy in the main building of the University of Technology on Karlsplatz. Nevertheless, this is the place in which to gain some understanding of Auer's sense of prestige. It is in this rarified atmosphere that he thrives and where he expends considerable effort to establish his credentials. On one occasion he arranges for an extraordinary wooden casket complete with drawers containing examples of work to be made to accompany his overview of printing processes. This summary is published under the name *Die Polygraphische Apparat*.

Apparently, the box survives. It is stored in the School of Graphic Media. There is no room in her schedule for such an expedition, but she will have to do something about that. It is not every day that you get a chance to inspect Auer's Polygraphic Apparatus.

The large windowless unit with yellow corrugated walls sits behind high fences on yet another industrial estate at the edge of town. In front of her are locked gates on which are various warnings – Achtung automatisches Tor, Achtung Quetschgefer, Fußgänger Verboten.

This is not Bradbury's legacy but it is fair to say that these days the Österreichische Staatsdruckerei (OeSD), a high-security printer, is not such a welcoming place. There is an entry phone system. Fortunately Pia has an appointment and passing through further security checks she is escorted to a waiting room where there is little option but to browse available material about OeSD's services, solutions and products. The company has been given clearance to work with classified material up to and including SECRET in accordance with EU security requirements. There is secure screening of suppliers and employees, secure material flow, monitored data deletion, secure spoilage management, secure distribution. There are additional levels of security – for example, no link (online or offline) between the production and administration departments; and 'every sub-process and every internal and external interface is examined from a security perspective'. This is a very safe place. Why does it make her feel nervous?

A young woman in a smart grey suit shows Pia to a characterless meeting room with a large glass table surrounded by tubular chairs and no pictures on the wall. A telephone, a jug of water, a glass. Also on the table are two large boxes designed to look like books and next to them are two copper plates. She will be given an overview of the company, then left to look through what remains from the old days. She may take photographs.

It seems that the Printing-office is still polygraphic, deploying many different technologies to prevent forgery and duplication; and doing clever things with paper and other substrates, with inks and with designs. Pia knows about special papers, about watermarks and security threads, but white light random fibres and chemical reagents are new to her. She knows inks can be special colours but is not familiar with iridescent ink, invisible fluorescent ink, or optically variable ink which displays two distinct colours depending on the angle from which it is viewed – a bit like the lenticular cards given away in boxes of cereal that show different images depending on how they are tilted. Unique numbering systems can be fluorescent or via barcodes or laser perforation. She learns about micro-lettering, see-through register (where images on both sides can be finely aligned), guilloches (complex engravings), latent images (that only appear when viewed through a special filter), transparent holographic overlays, prismatic colouring (rainbow printing), ghost images (seen using a lens with a specific screen ruling); and chip-related features containing biometric information. Printing here is sophisticated and varied and the firm's success still depends on its expertise in the application of innovative techniques. Furthermore, it occurs to her that biometric information – fingerprint recognition, iris scans, palm veins and so on – is a form of nature-printing. This innovative approach seems a vindication of Auer's career.

* * *

The loose-leaf albums on the table at the OeSD contain a fine collection of prints, highlights of the nature-printing season. Here, for the gentlemen of the Austrian Chamber of Commerce, is a fine array of lace specimens on blue ground, plus a couple of unsuccessful white-on-white blind-embossed versions. Here are prints of snakeskin, each scale picked out in gentle relief against the page, and here are the petrified fish that so impressed the jury at the Great Exhibition. There are also many examples of the work of Ettingshausen and Pokorny and these take her by surprise. Seen individually rather than bulk-bound in monumental tomes, she realises just how beautifully arranged on the page each plant is; how careful the shaping of stems, how precise the individual placing of petals to give the best impression of a flower. These specimens have been prepared by people who are fully aware of the objectives, rather than by a printer in a hurry. On other prints available here, where the flowers are in colour, the results are as good. She examines the detail and vibrant colour of small mosses and other cryptogams, then runs her finger over the prints to feel their familiar springy texture. It is a pleasure to step back from the tangled politics of those times and enjoy such inspiring work.

The two copper plates are of the same page from *Naturselbstdruck*, of three plants in flower, printed in at least five colours. One is the intermediate, or 'mother plate', similar to those seen at the Botanical Institute, with the image in relief. The other is a final intaglio printing plate, the first of its kind she has seen, still attached to the two hooked copper strips that would have held it in suspension in the electrolyte. The backs of both plates and the hooks have been coated with a yellow latex to prevent copper forming there. Pia puts the prints back in their book-boxes and the grey-suited woman appears almost instantly to escort her from the premises.

Bradbury delivers a lecture *On the Security and Manufacture of Bank Notes* to the Royal Institution on May 9, 1856, a talk illustrated with examples of banknotes signed by Henry Bradbury rather than by the Chief Cashier. While Bradbury still had plans for nature-printing, there has been a shift in priorities prompted by the chance to make some real money. His new venture, Bradbury and Wilkinson, is a success with customers all over the world. Like the OeSD it prints postage stamps, passports and identity documents – and it also has a licence to print money. More than a century later, in 1986, it is taken over by De La Rue (the company whose founder had recommended Bradbury to Auer, now the largest commercial banknote printer in the world).

According to Bradbury, the security printer must aim 'to stamp upon the production an *individuality* expressing qualities which are not within the province of mechanical reproduction'. The unique qualities of the nature-print would have been well-suited to such a project. Did it ever occur to Bradbury to combine security and nature-printing? After all, as Roderick Cave explains, it worked in 1738 for Benjamin Franklin. In Franklin's secret procedure:

> ...the leaf would be forced down into the surface of the cloth, and the threads of the cloth would show through the surface of the leaf. When all had dried, this would be brushed very lightly with oil, and a negative cast taken from it. When this had hardened, liquid type metal would be poured on to the prepared surface of the negative cast...the metal revealed a replica with all the veining of the leaf and the texture of the cloth, in a way which was almost impossible to copy...

Imagine the sophistication that Bradbury might have brought to this business. Instead, a specimen book of clip-art for banknotes was produced in 1860. It shows various guilloche borders, lettering and engravings for 'the attention of Merchants and Bankers of all Countries, as the result of the combination of artistic design and improved machinery used (exclusively) in the Engraving of Bank Notes, by Henry Bradbury, Bank Note Manufacturer'. (The designer for Bradbury's first notes was the same John Leighton who designed the commemorative shield for the Great Exhibition, an ornament set up in electrotype by Elkington.) This book demonstrates a reliance on the excellence of traditional skills. New methods are also being developed for security printing and here Bradbury applies the strategy that had succeeded against Vienna. He claims to have developed zinc-coated engraving plates for the long runs required for banknotes, even though the concept had been patented already by someone else. While the Pretsch/Talbot affair illustrates how difficult things can be at the cutting edge of technology in a fiercely inventive age, this is different; a bizarre episode revealing much about Bradbury's state of mind.

He chooses to announce in the *Journal of the Society of Arts* (February 4, 1859) the details of a new 'mode of surfacing engraved copper-plates with a coating of pure zinc by electro-metallurgical means, for the purpose of protecting such plates from wear when printing'. It is presented as a purely benevolent act 'for the benefit of those interested in extending the application of the galvano-plastic art'. We learn how to obtain a deposit of zinc on a plate that is 'capable of printing 1500 to 2000 impressions, or more'. (This doesn't sound significant given that the plates for web-offset today will stand a million impressions and those on gravure presses are good for much longer runs, but Bradbury's contemporaries are best-placed to judge the benefit of using zinc.) Mr Joubert, a French national living in London, points out coating plates with iron rather than zinc makes them much more durable, 'capable of yielding 10,000 impressions and upwards before the coating shows the first signs of wear'. Joubert also mentions that

Bradbury's new idea is actually 'an imitation of the process of covering engraved copper-plates with iron before sending them to the press' which he, Joubert, has patented and given the name 'acierage'. The modest tenor of Joubert's reply allows Bradbury the chance to admit to an honest mistake. This is not Bradbury's way. A robust response had worked for him in the past:

> Sir – It is a tolerably well-known fact among those conversant with electro-metallurgy as applied to printing purposes, that copper-plates have, since many years, been coated with silver and gold, for the purpose of protecting the plate from wear while being printed.

In other words, Joubert's idea is not original. He is simply copying others. To at least one nature-printer, this must have had a familiar ring. Bradbury goes on to say:

> The fact is that in this, as in most matters of a similar kind, adaption is mistaken for invention. M Joubert has undoubtedly by his *acquired* process greatly improved the practical means of a system sufficiently well-known to *practical* men…but I believe it is a great mistake to ascribe to M Joubert…the full honour of an original invention.

In addition to gold, silver and zinc, nickel, palladium and platinum – and iron – were also suitable for covering engraved plates, according to Bradbury. There is a swaggering assurance to his account that is utterly convincing and only one small problem: he is wrong. A baffled correspondent asked Bradbury to 'state any instances' of gold, silver or other metals being used to coat plates 'for the information of those, who, like myself, are unacquainted with the fact'. Joubert wonders mildly if Bradbury:

in order to screen himself from imitation…brings forward a counter-charge against me of having copied others, on the startling assumption "it is a well-known fact that gold and silver have for many years been used for coating plates to protect them from wear while being printed."

This is contrary to facts and all the printers with whom I have acquaintance, after being consulted, will bear testimony that Mr Bradbury is in complete error; that there was a great desideratum for some means of protecting engraved copper plates from wearing away as they do while at printing, and that the principal houses in London, Messrs McQueen, Messrs Brookes and others hailed with great satisfaction the introduction of my process.

Joubert may be a foreigner but he is popular and on good terms with local printers. All of a sudden it is horribly clear that, in making claims for a mechanism he does not understand, the hubristic Bradbury is out of his depth and will not be able to bluster through. Joubert finishes with a crushing blow:

Before retiring from this controversy, into which I have been forced, much against my habits and my wish, I shall only say briefly that, being taunted by Mr Bradbury with what he is pleased to call my *acquired* process, I readily acknowledge that I have acquired it by the most legitimate and fair means.

We hear no more on the subject from Bradbury, but a deeper silence follows as the implicit meaning of Joubert's final flourish sinks in. There is indeed a parallel to be drawn between this case and the nature-printing debacle and if one is a case of brazen opportunism, then the inference is clear. No wonder Bradbury backed off. In dealing with Vienna we saw him at the height of his powers, an indomitable chancer nervelessly marshalling an array of convincing arguments that made the more experienced Auer seem foolish. Here, in contrast, we have an impetuous, shambolic character with an insupportable confidence. A soapbox hoaxer. Bradbury, it seems, is in bad shape.

Pia has a plane to catch but first must visit Höhere Graphische Bundes-Lehr-und Versuchsenstalt (the School of Graphic Media) which has the appearance of a sixth-form college. There is a trade fair in progress and the people on the door assume that she has come to see a demonstration of modern printing methods. Of course this is exactly the reason, it's just that she is a hundred and sixty-five years too late. People are milling in groups and it is hard to find her way. A student offers vague directions. After a helter-skelter dash through corridors she bursts in to a small office. The man behind the desk looks up and raises an eyebrow. Her momentum has taken Pia half-way across the room and a smooth exit is impossible, but she does her best to apologise and escape.

'What are you looking for?' When she explains the object and urgency of her visit, the man springs out of his chair.

'But this is preposterous! I am probably the only person in the building who knows about the Polygraphic Apparatus.'

His name is Klaus Walder. He is a lecturer who has recently finished his thesis at the Institute of Art History in Vienna, on the history and archives of the Staatsdruckerei. They head for the library and draw a blank on the computer catalogue. Klaus marches to a cabinet of index files and after some rummaging pulls out a pink card. What they are looking for is in the basement. 'Unbelievable,' he mutters, as they clatter down several flights of stairs to a large general store-room of box-files, planning-chests and tables. They are aimed for the far corner and come to an abrupt stop in front of a large Xerox. 'Un-believ-able,' says Klaus, again. The most mundane of office machines, a redundant photocopier, stands in their way. After a brief struggle he retrieves a box ('Bananas, Certified Organic') containing what at first glance appears to be a large red book.

'This is a kunstkabinett, a wunderkammer,' says Klaus.

It is smaller than expected. When the lid (if this *was* a book, it would be the front cover) is lifted a tray inlaid with blue velvet is revealed, in which are inset 'galvanic' casts of medals, coins and cameos. Below are shallow, tight-fitting trays for metal-edged prints and copper plates and type specimens in foreign alphabets. Here are now-familiar examples of Naturselbstdruck: lace, a flowering plant that Pia cannot identify; and an oak leaf. Relief and intaglio versions of the plate are provided. There are examples of Leydolt's mineralographie, the etched agates and petrified fish, and prints produced by a wide variety of different processes such as chemitypie and xylographie. Another drawer holds the faded photograph of St Stephan's cathedral taken from the architect's window; the work of the retoucher is apparent on roofs in the foreground. Here is a photograph of a silk-worm breaking out of its egg, 'three thousand times larger than nature'. There are productions of the guilloche machine, steel and copperplate engravings, lithographs, even woodcuts. This is indeed a cabinet of curiosities and it says much about the history of printing and the graphic arts.

The fact that it is stored in a banana box in the basement also says something about the history of printing. A timely reminder that her purpose is to make prints.

As speculation over a suicide is no more than gossip, feel free to step over the next few paragraphs – particularly if you are an admirer of Dickens. A credible hypothesis to account for Bradbury's self-destruction is romantic rejection by one of the daughters of his father's partner, Frederick Mullett Evans. If true, Bradbury expert Adrian Dyer has deduced the daughter in question is Margaret Moule Evans, who married Richard Orridge on August 21, 1860. Eleven days later Bradbury took his own life. With reference to the theory Charles Dickens remarked that it was highly unlikely 'whether any blurred vision of that most undesirable female with the brass-headed eyes ever crossed his drunken mind'.

Though there is consilience between the remarks of Dickens and Auer, what is striking is the unpleasantness of Dickens' tone. Only a few years earlier, Dickens had been 'moved to have had poor [William] Bradbury's note' about the death of Little Nell in *The Old Curiosity Shop*; for he knew William (Henry's father) had lost a daughter, Letitia, to consumption. The change of mood can be ascribed to a bitter split with his publisher (Bradbury & Evans) following its reasonable refusal to print Dickens' justification for his separation from his wife Catherine on the basis that a 'comic miscellany' like *Punch* is not the place for 'statements on a domestic and painful subject'. This stance cost them dearly. They never published another of his works. Dickens never again spoke to William Bradbury and refused to attend the wedding of his son Charley to Bessie Evans because the reception was to be held at Evans' house (though later, when Bessie gave birth to a daughter, the young family was permitted to visit Gad's Hill). And Dickens gloated over the death of Bradbury's son, though he had the decency to alter his name to Simpson:

this young man…offered to make oath "wot he dun it in Cremorne in a bottle o' Soda Water. It wos last Sunday, wot he knowed Mr. Simpson well, and he dun it there"…the wretched creature is doubtless dead.

Dickens noted that 'nothing having appeared in the papers, I suppose strong influence to have been used in that wise, to keep the dismal story quiet'. Such may have been the intention, but it is not quite true. A version of the story was published in *The Belfast News-Letter* on Wednesday, September 12, 1860.

> The late Mr. William [sic] Bradbury, a junior partner in the firm of Bradbury, Evans & Co., the eminent printers and publishers, of Fleet Street, whose death, 'suddenly', appeared in the London journals on Saturday, committed suicide under very distressing circumstances. In consequence of the feud between Mr. C. Dickens and the senior partners in the firm, a matrimonial engagement, was, it is said, broken off between the late Mr. Bradbury and a daughter of Mr. Dickens, which preyed so much upon the mind of the unfortunate gentleman that he put an end to his existence. It is also stated that he had, unknown to his family, contracted some pecuniary obligations, which added materially to aggravate his position. Mr. William [sic] Bradbury was extremely well-looking, his prospects were good, and he was about the last person in the world who would be suspected of terminating his existence by a violent death.

A couple of days later there is a follow-up article in the same news-letter that corrects the mistake in the first (Henry, not William) but adds another, praising Bradbury's 'magnificent specimens' of 'chromolithography' in *Nature-Printed Ferns*. It is hard to know what to make of such errors. Even official notices of Bradbury's death, like the one printed in *The Morning Post* and elsewhere, were not fault-free:

Bradbury – On the 1st inst., suddenly, aged thirty-one, Henry, eldest son of Mr. William Bradbury of Whitefriars.

At his death, Henry Bradbury was only thirty years old; the slip was taken to his gravestone. The connection between Bradbury and Dickens' eldest daughter Mamie is interesting because it is known she did receive a proposal of marriage rejected by her father because he deemed the match unsuitable. Mamie never married and the suitor's identity has remained a mystery.

* * *

The plane circles once over Vienna then swings away. Pia can't resist looking back one more time at Auer and Bradbury. From this distance certain landmarks and major routes are clear, while details are unfathomable. Here is Auer, clear as a city. His printing-office sparkles in the late-afternoon sun. See the paper mill, the porcelain factory, the shining road to another print factory at Lvov. Big responsibilities, yet he lacks influence. In a court of landowning nobility and bureaucrats, the newly knighted self-made man is neither one thing nor the other and therefore, he has no friends. He must learn the meaning of euphemisms: adjustment, economies, downsizing. Once cost-saving is the prevailing philosophy, a business is lost. He must preside over the diminution of the Printing-office, the loss of confidence and ambition, the surrender of the field. In 1868, Auer throws in the towel in disgust. One year later, he is dead.

If the Empire had been in better shape, or if Brück had survived in office, might the future of nature-printing have been different? Over time, Auer's focus of attention might have switched to other processes. In a polygraphic institute like the one he built at Vienna, new ideas emerge regularly. The trick is to welcome innovations, give them a fair chance to develop and see what happens. Auer was good at this. All the same it is easy to wonder about those lost works, the ones that were never commissioned. That plans for nature-printing were shelved and then forgotten is a matter for regret – like the premature death of an artist – because the Naturselbstdruck of the Staatsdruckerei did represent a union of scientific, technical and artistic expertise.

The light fails as they approach England and the landscape is indistinct. Bradbury is a very different place to Auer but from a distance there may be similarities. For instance, there is an assumption that he experiences financial difficulties attempting to commercialise a process so costly it is abandoned in Austria. Perhaps so, though costs are not necessarily comparable in each case. Big companies tend to find the most expensive methods of production. New nature-printed publications do not appear on schedule and *The Nature-Printed Seaweeds* includes fewer prints than advertised, though this may simply indicate that priorities change as the result of the development of the banknote enterprise. The gossipy *Belfast News Letter*'s obituary suggests that by 1860 Bradbury had 'contracted pecuniary obligations' but how much credit is it possible to give an article that doesn't even get his name right?

Bradbury does at least have plans to develop what he calls the 'Octavo Series of Nature-Printed Works' and his list includes British trees (native and exotic), exotic ferns, mosses, lichens, British grasses and forage plants, British weeds and wild flowers, hepaticae – liverworts and scale mosses. Authors are lined-up for each book. An exciting and impressive list, though there are doubts about the probable quality of the series, given *The Octavo Book of Nature-Printed British Ferns* is not a brilliant effort in comparison with its larger cousin. This is a moot point, since none of the projects sees the light of day. Moreover, many hold that the octavo-sized *The Nature-Printed Seaweeds* exhibits the finest nature-prints. For Pia, though, the first book on ferns, a work of which Bradbury was justifiably proud, is hard to beat. He sent out copies to heads of state, perhaps with half-an-eye to the prospects of patronage. Letters of gratitude were received from Queen Victoria, the Pope and the King of Sweden. The King of Prussia awarded him a gold medal and the Tsar of Russia, a diamond ring. With characteristic self-assurance Bradbury also despatched a presentation copy to the Emperor of Austria and was presumably amused to obtain a positive response. Did he send a book to Auer?

On the face of it these were good times. A series of books in the pipeline and the development of a separate, potentially complementary line of trade. The public quibble over acierage is surely soon forgotten. At the end of the decade Bradbury leaves a comfortable responsible position in the family firm to pursue the burgeoning banknote business that will outlive Bradbury & Evans. The motive behind this bold move is unclear, since he might have been expected to succeed his father at the helm of the company but Bradbury is well-connected and apparently has many friends in the publishing world. Not many of us would want to be judged on the basis of what we do for a living and it should not be a surprise to learn that the few scraps of work-related information we have, which suggest an ostensibly successful career at the leading edge of print-publishing, offer little insight into the state of mind of the individual. Henry Bradbury's death in 1860, whether for love or for money, seals the fate of nature-printing in Britain. The facts of Bradbury's demise are few. The death certificate gives Bradbury's profession as 'bank note engraver'; a further sign of the road that might have been taken. Cause of death: 'suicide with prussic acid. Mind unsound.' The location is given as Cremorne Gardens, Chelsea.

The plane is on its final descent following the line of the Thames. Below is Chelsea Physic Garden and just a few hundred metres further on, in the shadow of the World's End estate tower blocks, is a modest green patch. This is Cremorne Gardens today. In Bradbury's time it was something else, a pleasure gardens with pageants, pyrotechnics, and prestidigitators; gas lights, concerts, dancing and 'no end of amusements'. Roll up, roll up! See a man being fired from a cannon. Admire the French female velocipedists. Marvel at the hot-air balloon ascents. Later in the evening the mood changed as, with a sure sense of Victorian melodrama, the petty criminals and prostitutes moved in. A Whistler painting from 1872, *Nocturne Blue and Silver Cremorne Lights*, showed the gardens from a distance; their fierce sparks reflected on the subdued stillness of an empty Thames under a leaden sky. This was the kind of place where things do not always go smoothly. On one occasion soldiers re-enacting a scene from the Crimean War fell on their bayonets when the stage they were on collapsed. Another time a hot-air balloon got impaled on a nearby church with a fatal outcome. And it is here, on September 1, 1860, after a fine day sharpened the air at dusk, while the gardens are ringing with the sounds of music, laughter and fireworks, that Bradbury raises a final toast to life with a glass of soda laced with poison.

At the 1862 International Exhibition, Paul Pretsch's photo-galvanographic plates were honoured with a medal. Bradbury & Evans displayed nature-prints and these were also awarded a prize; though it was only a retrospective, of little consequence; nature-printing in Britain had, it seems, reached the end of the line.

Working from pictures and notes and descriptions and telephone conversations, James at the electroplating firm is able to provide a plate (of a large oak leaf) identical to those seen in Vienna. An invoice that arrives by separate post serves to remind Pia that both Bradbury and Auer were probably brought down by the high costs associated with the operation. It seems she will be able to afford to make only a limited number of nature-prints. Through James's generosity she is able to secure a significant discount but this cannot be relied on in the future.

But she has two plates! The test-plate boater hat (now filled with Tiranti's epoxy) and a beautiful and precious silvered copper panel wrapped in tissue paper. She puts both in her pannier and is soon pedalling furiously across London to catch the Reading train.

* * *

A few days later, Pia sits watching Rosie inspect the first prints with the concentration of a connoisseur. The single large oak leaf has come out well.

'How long did you say it takes to make each one?'

Pia can't help laughing because she has explained already that each print represents more than an hour's labour as a direct result of her inexperience in inking and wiping the plate. Rosie shakes her head, says how much she likes the results, then murmurs a gentle question about plans. To make plans still feels optimistic, even though she has reached a position from which she can start to work with a proper plate – at least this time she is just about ready to begin. This realisation forces her to wonder why nature-printing ever seemed like a good idea. She does her best not to frown at Rosie. It is the seductive power of the image that must bear responsibility. Isn't it always the way? The Austrian

Chamber of Commerce was persuaded by the images of lace it saw at the Great Exhibition – but commerce rarely commissioned a printed lace sample book. Scientists were convinced initially that the method could be used for plants and fossils, a decision once again made on the strength of the quality of images – but botanists and paleobiologists did not take the principle very far, either.

These days no-one believes in the idea of an objective image. So we are left with an innovative technical process driven by industry, admired by science, abandoned by both. Why did all the grand plans fail to materialise? Was it dropped simply because it was costly, limited, slow, difficult? Was it for such good and trivial reasons that the over-hyped underachiever was consigned to the Printing Historical Society's file of curiosities? The Scythian lamb that turned out to be a woolly fern[1]. So be it. In spite of its comprehensive defeat the unsurpassed quality of the image shines through, magnificent in its own unsuccess, and Pia wants to carry on. There is a value in what has been lost. This is the essence of alchemy, like the transformation of something as heavy and dull and malleable as stamped lead into something else entirely. The short-term problem is that nature-printing is still difficult, slow and also very costly. She explains to Rosie that she would like to make at least one full-size fern print, perhaps some flowers, some leaves, then experiment with a view to making something entirely

---

1 *Cibotium barometz* was listed in 1975 in the category of controlled trade species in Appendix II of CITES (The Convention on International Trade in Endangered Species). It is used for medicinal purposes in parts of South East Asia, where it is deemed beneficial for liver and kidney function, for the treatment of rheumatism and backache, and (as Elizabeth Blackwell knew) as a blood coagulant. The fern is not cultivated, so harvesting of this rather slow-growing plant is from the wild population; though widespread, it is thought to be in serious decline. Since 1997, the China CITES office has prohibited export of the plant, known locally as Jinmao Gou (Golden Hair Dog Fern) and Huanggoutou (Yellow Dog's Head Fern).

new; inspired by but somehow different from, the work of Auer and Bradbury.

'I'm glad to hear that bats don't form part of your plan.'

It is supposed to be a joke but it reminds her once again of the parable. Most people have no conception of what nature-printing is and she feels rather alone. And she cannot afford to make enough different prints to promote her approach, or see how it will ever be possible to build her own electroforming studio; and at this moment both seem equally unlikely. Rosie, like Michael Hayward before her, suggests appealing for subscribers for fern prints in the Fern Society's magazine. This a good idea but it will not carry her far.

'Why not write a book about your rediscovery of nature-printing – a tale of industrial espionage, ferns and roofing lead? It is an object lesson in persistence. Or perhaps you might find someone crazy enough to write it for you.'

'I think I will,' Pia replies.

Pia has rented space in a small studio near her home and she sets to work. She makes prints. She finds better-quality inks and develops a precise colour chart for reference purposes. With the help of Ian, who runs the studio, she improves her technique of inking and cleaning the plate. There's just one thing. She only has one good plate, so all her prints are of the same leaf. It has become a stock joke: is she planning on making a tree? what colour, today? has she considered a fluorescent oak leaf?

To have cracked the process only to be stifled by economic considerations is frustrating. It is imperative to overcome her reluctance to make plates. Ian is encouraging and supportive and she begins to explore seriously the possibility of building her own plate-making facility. The notes from her session with Simon in Leeds are useful. She can refer to a range of books. By now she knows one or two practical people. Electroplating is not a big mystery. There are some – jewellers and folk who like to tinker with cars – who are familiar with the subject. Starter sets suitable for plating small items are available on eBay, though Pia is working on a larger scale. Slowly, she pieces things together. An aquarium, a pump, a rectifier to enable a DC-regulated power supply. Hard to know what the level of power should be: too high and the copper will ripple, too low and it will not stick. She is delighted to discover a supplier of sulphuric acid, but is thrown when asked what concentration of acid she requires. Formulating a recipe for the solution is a big challenge and another supplier corrects her list of ingredients, suggesting two hundred grams of copper sulphate might be better than two grams. A filter bag, liquid latex for the back of the plate, brightening agent to make the plate shiny. A bar of copper to act as the anode. And silly things: a wooden spoon for stirring; crocodile clips. Finally, she is ready to begin. Ian works with her, offering practical suggestions like 'don't put de-ionised water in the acid, there might be a reaction; instead, add acid to the water'. Such familiarity with chemicals is reassuring and there is a level of confidence about his approach that is infectious. When it proves difficult to solder thick copper wire to the back of the lead plate using the circuit-board soldering iron Pia has bought, Ian fires up a blowtorch. Meanwhile, she sets up the small aquarium heater. It takes ages to raise the bucket-load of distilled water to the correct temperature. All preparations are undertaken with a level of urgency and a quiet, irrepressible excitement which may be no more than the energy that comes from making things, a rare experience in these ready-made, pre-packed times.

The intense copper sulphate blue of the tank makes it almost impossible to see what is happening. There is no dramatic fizz. After forty-five minutes the power is switched off and the plate lifted up. Look there, on the edge of the plate! What is that? It is the excitement of a scientist at Cern. Eventually, Pia leaves the studio for the night. Twenty-four restless hours later, the power is switched off again. What emerges from the blue solution is a bright copper plate. Interesting how the copper has grown like coral beyond the edges of the lead. On the surface of the plate it is smooth. Show it to us.

ACKNOWLEDGEMENTS

The book would not have been possible without Pia Östlund. I am very grateful for her support. Adrian Dyer, who knows more about Henry Bradbury than anyone, was generous with information on the subject. Michael Hayward very kindly provided many of the featured images. In some places, Michael's own collection has been exaggerated. He does not own Henry Smith's work and pointed out that a similar book, a hand-coloured Hunziker (*Nature's Self-Printing*, Managalore, 1862) sold recently for £40,000. The photographer Andrew Montgomery gave permission to use his work. Sue Purcell managed somehow to decipher the gothic type of *Mein Dienstleben*. Patrick at The Fine Bindery provided expert advice and encouragement. Caroline Bateman, field botanist, allowed me to accompany her on enjoyable expeditions. Yuri Gavrilov edited the pictures. Pam Bains helped in many ways, as is usually the case. Finally, there is Miranda, who checked the text carefully and helped in so many other ways – this book is for you.

SP

First and most of all I would like to thank Tim Preston for suggesting this collaboration and for the enthusiasm, skill and wit with which Simon Prett turned my rambling account, disparate notes, and photographs into a coherent story which captures the spirit of the project. His own research and contributions to the subject matter should not be underestimated. I am thankful for all the kindnesses I've been shown along the way. I am ever grateful to Rosie Atkins for introducing me to Chelsea Physic Garden and its library in the first place and to Linda Forrest for seeing this book project through. Other supportive friends at the Garden include Gillian Barlow and Liz Thornton. I am indebted to Professor Michael Twyman and the Typography Department, University of Reading for the expertise and guidance they bestowed on the project. The Printing Historical Society and the Swedish Embassy contributed much-needed funds, which helped with the research. Eric Hochberg pointed me in the direction of the copper plates in Vienna. Rod Cave offered helpful advice and I have had many useful exchanges with both Michael Hayward and Adrian Dyer. Transatlantic art writer and editor Kyra Kordoski also deserves a special mention. Many institutions and librarians played an invaluable part in offering assistance and access to their collections. In Vienna: Maren Gröning at the Albertina, Stefan Sienell at the Austrian Academy of Sciences, Matthias Svojtka at the Botany Library and Klaus Walder at die Graphische; in Copenhagen and London: Design Museum Denmark, St Bride Library, the Linnean Society, the Natural History Museum, the Royal Institution and the Wellcome Collection to mention a few. Ian Steadman of Arcane studios taught me how to edition and ink a la poupée and Chris Roantree helped man the electroforming tanks out of hours.

I also would like to thank my parents for their love and kindness (and for allowing their bookshelves to be turned into a giant flower press). The pressed plant in this book was brought back from Swedish woods close by their place, Hult in Småland. Last but not least, to John for all his good thoughts and to my best friends Laure and Stephen for always being there: thank you.

PÖ

Bibliography

AITKEN, W C, 1866. *The Early History of Brass and the Brass Manufacturers of Birmingham.* Birmingham.

'AMC' (COLE, Allan), 1880. *A Guide to Nature-Printing Butterflies and Moths.* London.

ALLEN, David Elliston, 1969. *The Victorian fern craze: a history of pteridomania.* London: Hutchinson.

AUER, Alois, 1851. *Geschichte der k. k. Hof- und Staats-Druckerei in Wien. Von einem Typographen dieser Anstalt.* Wien.

AUER, Alois, 1853. *Die Entdeckung des Naturselbstdruckes. The discovery of the natural printing process.* Wien: Aus der kaiserlich-königlichen Hof- und Staatsdruckerei.

AUER, Alois, 1853. *The Polygraphic Apparatus, or, the different departments of art carried on in the Imperial Court and Government Printing-office at Vienna.* Vienna.

AUER, Alois, 1923. *Mein Dienstleben.* Wien, Leipzig.

AUSTRIA, Staatsdruckerei, 1853. *Naturselbstdruck (aus der k. k. Hof- und Staatsdruckerei zu Wien. Pflanzen, Blumen und Blätter; Geätzte Steine; Moose; Spitzen und Stoffe; Versteinerungen; Verschiedenes).* Wien.

BARRET, Oliver, 2007. *A history of the Woodburytype : the first successful photo-mechanical printing process and Walter Bentley Woodbury.* Nevada City, California: Carl Mautz Pub.

BLACKWELL, Elizabeth, 1737. *A Curious Herbal containing five hundred cuts of the most useful plants, which are now used in the practice of physick, to which is added a short description of ye plants and their common uses in physick.* London: Samuel Harding.

BRADBURY, Henry Riley, 1847. *Reminiscences of a visit to Chatsworth.* London: Bradbury & Evans.

BRADBURY, Henry Riley, 1856. *Nature printing: its origin and objects. A lecture delivered at the Royal Institution, May 11, 1855.* London: Bradbury & Evans.

BRADBURY, Henry Riley, 1860. *Specimens of Bank Note Engraving &c. &c. &c. Designed & Executed by Henry Bradbury.* London.

BRADBURY, Henry, 1854. *A few leaves represented by "Nature-Printing," showing the application of the art for the reproduction of botanical and other natural objects, etc.* London.

BRADBURY, Henry, 1855. *Nature printing: a technical process for obtaining printed reproduction of plants and other objects, natural and artificial.* London: Bradbury & Evans.

BRADBURY, Henry, 1856. *On the Security and Manufacture of Bank Notes. A lecture.* London: Bradbury & Evans.

BRADBURY, Henry. 1858. *Printing: its Dawn, Day & Destiny.* London: Bradbury & Evans.

BRADBURY, Henry. 1860. *Autotypography, or, Art of nature-printing.* London. (see Dyer, AF).

Camus, JM (Ed), 1991. *The History of British Pteridology*, 1891-1991. London: British Pteridological Society.

Cave, Roderick and Wakeman, Geoffrey, 1967. *Typographia naturalis*. Wymondham: Brewhouse Press.

Cave, Roderick, 2010. *Impressions of Nature, A History of Nature Printing*. London: The British Library.

Daston, Lorraine and Galison, Peter, 2010. *Objectivity*. New York: Zone Books.

Davy, Elizabeth, 1831. *Butterflies and moths*. NHM Collection.

Dawtry Drewitt, F, 1924. *The Romance of the Apothecaries' Garden at Chelsea*. London and Sydney: Chapman and Dodd.

Dyer, Adrian 1987. *Nature Printing especially in Ferns*. NHM archives.

Dyer, AF, 2015. *The Life and Craft of William and Henry Bradbury, Masters of Nature Printing in Britain*. (Includes extracts from *Autotypography* – see Bradbury, above). Publication impending: Huntia; www.huntbotanical.org/

Eder, Josef Maria, 1945. *History of Photography*. London: Constable.

Edgington, John, 2013. *Who Found Our Ferns?* London: British Pteridological Society.

Endlicher, Stephan , 1844. *Endlicher's Paradisus Vindbonensis*. Wien.

Ettingshausen, Constantin and Pokorny, Alois, 1856-73. *Physiotypia plantarum Austriacarum... .* Wien. (Prague.)

Faber, Monika, 2008. *Urban Panoramas, Photographs of the Imperial and Government Printing Establishment*, 1850-1860. Vienna: Albertina.

Farre, Arthur, 1851. *Collection of Nature Prints of South European butterflies and moths*. London: Entomology library, nhm.

Fortune, Robert, 1852. *A journey to the tea countries of China : including Sung-lo and the Bohea Hills : with a short notice of the East India Company's tea plantations in the Himalaya Mountains*. London: John Murray.

Fry, Carolyn, 2009. *The Plant Hunters*. London: Andre Deutsch.

Gribbin, Mary and John, 2008. *Flower Hunters*. New York: oup.

Guettier, A, 1872. *A Practical Guide for the Manufacture of Metallic Alloys*. London: Sampson Low, Son & Marston.

Hall, Nigel and Rickard, Martin, 2006. *Fern Books*. London: British Pteridological Society.

Harris, Elizabeth M, 1968-1970. Experimental Graphic Processes in England, 1800-1859. London: *Journal of the Printing Historical Society*; Printing Historical Society.

Hatcher, J and Barker, T C, 1974. *A History of Bristish Pewter*. London: Longman.

Hayward, Michael, 2015. *The Jones Nature Prints. Nature Printing and the Victorian Fern Cult*. London: British Pteridological Society.

Heilmann, P, 1982. *Die Natur als Drucker*. Dortmund: Harenberg.

Holding, Andy and Moulson, David. 1994. *Pewtering in Bewdley*. Upton-Upon-Severn: Wyre Forest District Council.

HULL, Charles, 1999. *Pewter*. Princes Risborough: Shire Publications.

HUME, Naomi, 2011. The Nature Print and Photography in the 1850s. *History of Photography*. London: Taylor & Francis.

JAY, Bill, 1988. *Walter Bentley Woodbury 1834-1885 and the history of his Woodburytype process*. PDF.

JELAVICH, Barbara, 1987. *Modern Austria: Empire and Republic, 1815-1986*. Cambridge: CUP

JOHNSTONE, William Grosart and CROALL, Alexander, 1859-1860. *The nature-printed British sea-weeds: a history, accompanied by figures and dissections of the Algae of the British Isles...nature printed by H Bradbury*. London: Bradbury & Evans.

JONES, Kathryn, 2010. 'To wed high art with mechanical skill': Prince Albert and the industry of art. London. V&A.

KNIGHT, Charles. 1858. *The English Cyclopædia*. London: Bradbury & Evans.

KNIPHOF, Johann Hieronymus, 1763. *Botanica in Originali seu Herbarium virum in quo plantarum... .* Halæ Magdeburgicæ.

LARSEN, Sonja, (Ed) 2011. *The art of printing from nature: A guidebook by the Nature Printing Society*. America: The Nature Printing Society.

LE ROUGETEL, Hazel, 1990. *The Chelsea Gardener, Philip Miller, 1691-1771*. London: British Museum.

MERRYWEATHER, James. 2007. *The Fern Guide*. Shrewsbury: FSC Publications.

MINTER, Sue, 2000. *The Apothecaries' Garden : a history of the Chelsea Physic Garden*. Stroud: Sutton.

MINTER, Sue. 1991. *The Chelsea Physic Garden. London*: Trustees of the Chelsea Physic Garden.

MOORE, Thomas, 1859. *The Octavo Nature-printed British Ferns... Nature-printed by H. Bradbury*. London. Bradbury & Evans.

MOORE, Thomas. 1855/6. *The Ferns of Great Britain and Ireland...edited by J Lindley. Nature-printed by H. Bradbury*. London: Bradbury & Evans.

MORAN, James, 1960. *Wynkyn de Worde*. London: Wynkyn de Worde Society.

MORTON, Sholto, Charles, Earl of, 1965. *The Chelsea Physic Garden*. London: Richard Madley.

ÖSTLUND, Pia, 2013. *The subjective nature of nature printing*. MA Dissertation, Reading.

PALMER, Alan. 1997. *Twilight of the Habsburgs: the life and times of Emperor Francis Joseph. London*: Phoenix Giant.

PARKINSON, Michael, 2007. *The Birmingham City Centre Masterplan: A Visioning Study*. Liverpool John Moores University: European Institute for Urban Affairs.

RICKARDS, Maurice, 2000. *Encyclopedia of Ephemera*. London: The British Library.

SCOTT, Jack L, 1980. *Pewter wares from Sheffield*. Baltimore: Antiquary Press.

SMITH, Henry, 1857. *Specimens of nature printing from unprepared plants*. Madras: H Smith at the Fort Saint George Gazette Press.

STANNARD, W J, 1859. *The Art-Exemplar; A Guide to Distinguish One Species of Print from Another, with Pictorial Examples and Written Descriptions of Every Known Style of Illustration.* London.

TAYLOR, A J P, 1981. *The Hapsburg Monarchy 1809-1918: a history of the Austrian Empire and Austria-Hungary.* Harmondsworth: Penguin, 1981.

TAYLOR, Roger, 2002, *Photographs Exhibited in Britain*, 1839-1865. Ottawa: National Gallery of Canada.

TIMMINS, Samuel, 1866. *The Resources, Products and Industrial History of Birmingham and the Midland Hardware District.* London: Robert Hardwicke.

TOMLINSON, Charles, 1854. *Cyclopædia of Useful Arts.* London: George Virtue & Co.

WAKEMAN, Geoffrey, 1983. *Victorian Book Illustration, The Technical Revolution.* Newton Abbot: David & Charles.

WALLIS, George, 1863. The New Art of Auto-Typography. *Journal of the Society of Arts.* London.

WHITTINGHAM, Sarah, 1997. 'Rambles Through Fernland': The Victorians' Passion for Ferns. *The Victorian.* London.

WEBB, Randall and REED, Martin, 1999. *Spirits of Salts.* London: Argentum.

WOOD, R Derek, 1975. The Calotype Patent Lawsuit of Talbot v Laroche, 1854. Bromley, Kent: R D Wood.

WEBSITES

www.pewtersociety.org

www.pewterers.org.uk

http://www.militarymetalwork.co.uk

http://www.alternativephotography.com

http://www.endodonziamauroventuri.it/Guttaperca/Historical%20 Uses%20of%20Gutta.pdf

http://foxtalbot.dmu.ac.uk/

http://fernalbums.co.uk